As they sea[rch] [for necta]r, bees pollina[te] [them. A b]ee uses its hairy body to pick up pollen from one flower and transfer it to another.

A worker bee will make only 1/12 of a teaspoon of honey and 1/80 of a tea-spoon of beeswax in her whole life.

Next time you pick a flower, eat an apple, or spread honey on your peanut butter sandwich, BE thankful for BEES! They're nature's sweeties.

Other books written by Kate Klise and illustrated by M. Sarah Klise:

Regarding the Fountain
Regarding the Sink
Regarding the Trees
Regarding the Bathrooms
Letters from Camp
Trial by Journal
Shall I Knit You a Hat?
Why Do You Cry?
Imagine Harry
Dying to Meet You

Also written by Kate Klise:

Deliver Us from Normal
Far from Normal

REGARDING THE BEES

A LESSON, IN LETTERS,
ON HONEY, DATING,
AND OTHER
STICKY SUBJECTS

KATE KLISE
ILLUSTRATED BY M. SARAH KLISE

sandpiper

HOUGHTON MIFFLIN HARCOURT
BOSTON   NEW YORK

Text copyright © 2007 by Kate Klise
Illustrations copyright © 2007 by M. Sarah Klise

The Library of Congress has catalogued the hardcover edition as follows:
Klise, Kate.
Regarding the bees: a lesson, in letters, on honey, dating, and other sticky subjects/
Kate Klise; illustrated by M. Sarah Klise.
p.   cm.
Summary: While corresponding with their globetrotting substitute teacher,
the seventh graders at Geyser Creek Middle School nervously prepare for
an important standardized test, navigate the tricky waters of first crushes,
and try to bring their bee mascot to a local spelling competition.
[1. Middle schools—Fiction.   2. Schools—Fiction.   3. Examinations—Fiction.
4. Letters—Fiction.   5. Humorous stories.]   I. Klise, M. Sarah, ill.   II. Title.
PZ7.K684Rd   2007
[Fic]—dc22   2006017716
HC ISBN-13: 978-0-15-205711-4 PA ISBN-13: 978-0-15-206668-0

Printed in the United States of America
DOC 10 9 8 7 6 5
4500377755

For Byron

"Books are the bees which carry the quickening pollen from one to another mind."

—James Russell Lowell

Sanitas per Aquas

GEYSER CREEK MIDDLE SCHOOL
Geyser Creek, Missouri

Mr. Walter Russ
Principal

September 8

Mr. Sam N.
Acting Principal
Geyser Creek Middle School
Geyser Creek, Missouri

Dear Mr. N.,

Thank you for agreeing to serve as principal while I'm away on special assignment this semester.

As you know, this is a critical semester for students at Geyser Creek Middle School. In December, all grades (5–8) will take the Basic Education Evaluation (BEE).

It's important that all of our students do well on this test, but particularly the seventh graders. Beginning this year, any seventh grader who fails the BEE must return to fifth grade immediately and begin middle school all over again.

Thank you and have a nice, quiet semester. I think that after you've spent a few months in my office, you'll agree that when it comes to being principal, silence is golden.

See you in January.

Walter Russ

Walter Russ

P.S. Good luck with the substitute you've chosen to teach your class. Maybe you'll have better luck communicating with her than I do.

Sam N.
Acting Principal
Geyser Creek Middle School
Geyser Creek, Missouri

OVERNIGHT MAIL

September 9

Florence Waters
President
Flowing Waters Fountains, Etc.
Watertown, California

Dear Florence,

This is the first letter I've written as principal. Seems fitting it should be to you.

I feel a bit overwhelmed by my new job. But I'm excited, too—almost as excited as my former students, who are now seventh graders. They're thrilled that you'll be teaching them this semester by correspondence course. Classes begin on September 12, so please send the first assignment.

I'll let the students tell you the bad news about the BEEs. I hope you can prepare them for this annual nightmare. Effective this year, the seventh graders *must* perform well on the BEEs—or else they have to repeat middle school.

I have lots of BEE preparation materials. Let me know if I should send them to you.

Sincerely,

Sam N.

Sam N.

P.S. One of the perks of this temporary job is getting to work with my honey, Goldie. Our baby is due exactly five months from today!

FLOWING WATERS FOUNTAINS, ETC.

Watertown, California

September 10

EXPRESS MAIL

Sam N.
Acting Principal
Geyser Creek Middle School
Geyser Creek, Missouri

Dear Sam,

You're making the children perform on BEEs? How very ODD.

I can tell you right now that I don't like the sound of this. But I'll wait to hear more from the seventh graders. They must be terrified.

I've enclosed the first assignment. Please unscroll and display on the blackboard for all to see. Then give Goldie and the baby-to-be a big hug from me.

Fondly,

H Florence

P.S. Thanks, Sam, but I don't need any BEE supplies. I have a whole barn full of equipment.

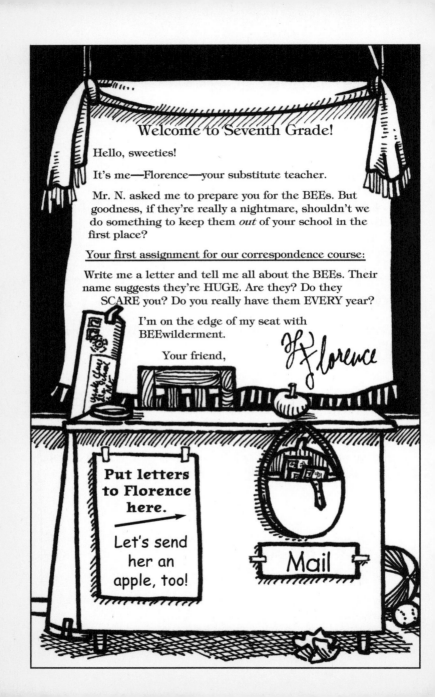

Welcome to Seventh Grade!

Hello, sweeties!

It's me—Florence—your substitute teacher.

Mr. N. asked me to prepare you for the BEEs. But goodness, if they're really a nightmare, shouldn't we do something to keep them *out* of your school in the first place?

<u>Your first assignment for our correspondence course:</u>

Write me a letter and tell me all about the BEEs. Their name suggests they're HUGE. Are they? Do they SCARE you? Do you really have them EVERY year?

I'm on the edge of my seat with BEEwilderment.

Your friend,

Florence

Put letters to Florence here. →

Let's send her an apple, too!

Mail

September 12

Florence Waters
Fountain Designer and Friend
Flowing Waters Fountains, Etc.
Watertown, California

Hello, Florence!

That was Lily. This is Paddy. Hi from me, too. Here's what we can tell you about the BEEs: They're the worst part of every school year.

We get the BEEs on the first Tuesday in December. They're really long. We have to spend all day on them. Just thinking about the BEEs gives me a headache.

I wish somebody could get rid of the BEEs, but they're what Mr. N. calls "a necessary evil."

Anyway, thanks for BEEing our substitute teacher this semester.

Lily   *Paddy*

P.S. Did you know it's a tradition at Geyser Creek Middle School that the seventh graders have a class dance on New Year's Eve? We don't want to. Dances are so old-fashioned and boring.

P.P.S. Besides that, we don't have boyfriends.

Seventh-Grade Correspondence Class
Geyser Creek Middle School
Geyser Creek, Missouri

September 12

Ms. Florence Waters
Our Substitute Teacher and *Permanent* Pal
Flowing Waters Fountains, Etc.
Watertown, California

Hi, Mizz Florence!

Thanks so much for agreeing to teach our class by writing letters back and forth. This is going to be the best semester ever!

Well, it would be except for the BEEs. Yes, we have them every year. They're a real pain in the BEEhind. I wish we could keep the BEEs out of our school, but we can't. There's a state law that says we have to tackle them every year.

Seventh graders also sponsor a New Year's Eve dance every year. Our class is going to take a vote to decide if we'll have one or not. Personally, I wouldn't mind having a dance—if I knew how to dance. I think I'll ask Mr. N. or Chef Angelo to teach me.

Of course I'd ask *you*, Florence. But I don't think you can teach me to dance in a letter.

Over and out for now.

Tad Poll

P.S. Guess what? I'm now working at the *Gazette* as a special correspondent.

Seventh-Grade Correspondence Class
Geyser Creek Middle School
Geyser Creek, Missouri

September 12

Florence Waters
Our Substitute Teacher and My Personal Hero
Flowing Waters Fountains, Etc.
Watertown, California

Hey there, Florence!

The BEEs are as terrible as they sound. I never do very well on them.

If you have any suggestions about how we can prepare for the BEEs, please don't BEE shy about telling us.

Speaking of shy . . . I'm sitting next to Gil this year. He was my boyfriend last year, but now he's really quiet around me. I don't know why. He has this totally cute buzz haircut. When I look at Gil, all I can think of is how _fun_ it's going to be to go to the New Year's Eve dance with him—and then I can't stop smiling!

Having a boyfriend makes school—and life—wonderful!

Sincerely,

Shelly

P.S. Don't worry about our class getting rowdy. Mr. N. said that if he can hear us from the principal's office, he'll bring in a local substitute teacher. Needless to say, we're all trying to be _very_ quiet.

7

September 12

Florence Waters
President of Flowing Waters Fountains, Etc.
Watertown, California

Dear Florence,

You asked if the BEEs are huge. Well, I can tell you this: They're a huge big deal. The worst part is we never know what's going to be on them.

On the day of the BEEs, teachers aren't allowed to help us even one tiny bit. If they do, the teacher gets fired and the student fails.

But here's a problem maybe you can help me solve: I'm sitting across from Gil. I've known him since kindergarten, but for some reason I feel really strange when I'm around him now—like I have butterflies in my stomach.

I'm trying not to look at him because I don't want to make Shelly mad. She's Gil's girlfriend. I'm sure they'll go to the New Year's Eve dance together—that is, if we even have a dance. I don't know if I want to if I can't go with Gil.

Is that terrible for me to think? And am I doing the right thing by ignoring Gil—even though I think I might like him?

I need advice, please.

Minnie O.

8

September 12

Florence Waters
Famous Designer and Substitute Teacher for Our Class
Flowing Waters Fountains, Etc.
Watertown, California

Hi, Florence.

I'm terrified of the BEEs. Last year I was so nervous, I got a
bad case of hives on the day of the BEEs. I did miserably. If I
don't perform well on them this year, I'll get sent back to
fifth grade.

The only thing I dread more than taking the BEE is talking
to girls. It doesn't help that I'm sitting across from Minnie O.,
the smartest girl in our class. I always thought she was
really nice, but this year she won't even look at me.

Meanwhile, Shelly is sitting right next to me. She's supposed
to be my girlfriend, but every time she looks at me, she
laughs. Probably because I've got this stupid short haircut.
Plus, I'm growing like crazy, but I'm not gaining any
weight. I look like a telephone pole with arms and legs.

I hope like heck we don't have a class dance. I get itchy just
thinking about it.

Bye for now.

Gil

P.S. We have a new custodian this year. Her name's Sugar
Kube. I keep saying hi to her, but she doesn't answer me.
I'm such a loser. What should I do?

Watertown, California

September 15

The Seventh-Grade Correspondence Class
Geyser Creek Middle School
Geyser Creek, Missouri

EXPRESS MAIL

Dearest class,

I've never heard of such big nasty BEEs!

The bees I know are tiny creatures with lovely habits, like
producing honey for our tea and beeswax for candles. It's
no exaggeration to say bees fill our world with sweetness
and light.

As proof, I'm sending you Honey, my beloved worker bee.
She's very intelligent. In fact, she can spell every word in
the *Oxford English Dictionary*. Do you mind caring for
Honey this semester? I think she might relieve some of
your BEE-related stress.

I've enclosed your next assignments. Please display on the
blackboard for all to read.

Yours sweetly,

Florence

P.S. I'm writing this by candlelight. Did you know I use
only beeswax candles to light my house?

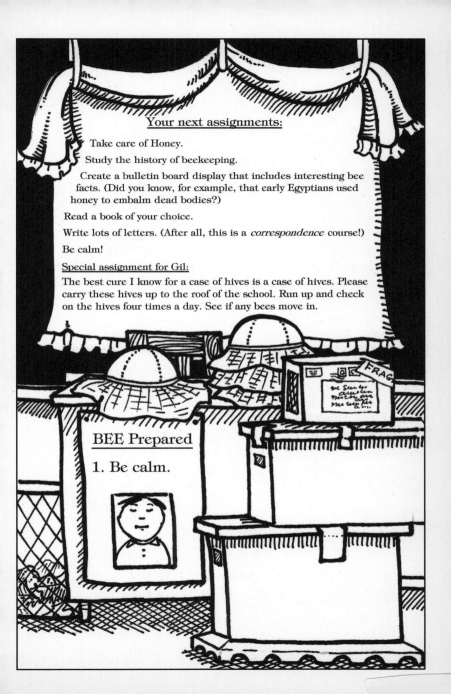

Your next assignments:

Take care of Honey.

Study the history of beekeeping.

Create a bulletin board display that includes interesting bee facts. (Did you know, for example, that early Egyptians used honey to embalm dead bodies?)

Read a book of your choice.

Write lots of letters. (After all, this is a *correspondence* course!)

Be calm!

Special assignment for Gil:

The best cure I know for a case of hives is a case of hives. Please carry these hives up to the roof of the school. Run up and check on the hives four times a day. See if any bees move in.

BEE Prepared

1. Be calm.

Even before recorded history, people gathered honey from bees living in hollow trees.

Ancient Egyptians made beehives by covering wicker baskets with clay and baking them in the sun until hard. Then they loaded the hives onto small rafts and floated them down the Nile.

Honey and bees were so important to the economy of Lower Egypt that a hieroglyph of the honeybee was the symbol of the entire region.

Honey was the first sweetener. It was so valued in early cultures that some people paid taxes with honey.

Egyptians used honey in their cooking, as medicine, and in religious ceremonies.

Egyptians also liked beeswax, which they used for mummification, shipbuilding, and as hair gel on their wigs!

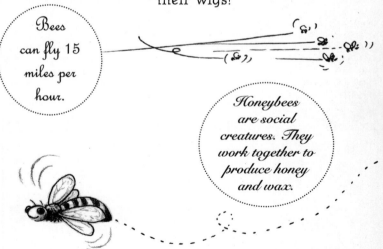

Bees can fly 15 miles per hour.

Honeybees are social creatures. They work together to produce honey and wax.

Honeybees are not native to North America. The first honeybees were brought to this country in the early 17th century by colonists.

★THE GEYSER CREEK GAZETTE★

Our motto: "We have a nose for news!"

Saturday, September 17   **Early Edition**   50 cents

Middle School Students Prepare for BEEs and Show-Me Bee

Across the state middle school students are preparing for the Basic Education Evaluation, commonly known as the BEE.

The BEE is a standardized test given on the first Tuesday of December to all Missouri middle school students. Not only do scores on these tests become part of a student's permanent record, BEE results are also closely monitored by the Missouri Department of Education. Schools that produce low BEE scores receive stinging criticism.

This year's BEE will be given on December 6.

Benny Bob "B. B." King, the director of the BEEs, said he is especially interested to see the test results from Springfield Middle School, which holds the record for the top BEE scores in the state.

Most BEE watchers credit Springfield Middle School teacher Polly Nader for her

B. B. King is BEE czar.

students' success. Last year her class scored highest in the state on the BEEs. In addition Nader's students won first place in last year's Show-Me Spelling Bee.

The Show-Me Spelling Bee is an invitation-only event. The winning school from the previous year selects the participating schools for the following year's competition.

"We'll be sending out invitations shortly," said Nader. "Bee prepared!"

Nader Predicted to Win HIVE Prize

Polly Nader is known as queen of the BEEs.

Springfield Middle School teacher Polly Nader is considered a shoo-in for the Highly Innovative and Victorious Educator (HIVE) Prize.

The HIVE Prize is given every 25 years by the Missouri Department of Education. Teachers are judged on their students' performance in the Show-Me Spelling Bee and on the Basic Education Evaluation (BEE). Letters of recommendation from students and

coworkers are also considered.

In addition to the prestige, the winner of the HIVE Prize receives a cash award of $1 million.

According to Melissa "Missy" Spelt, executive director of the Missouri Department of Education and judge of the HIVE Prize competition, Nader has already received more than 2,000 letters of recommendation from her students.

"Oh, I wouldn't know about that," said Nader. "My job is not to win prizes but to instill in students a love of learning. That's the real reward of teaching."

Geyser Creek Seventh Graders Receive "Honey" of a Package

By Tad Poll, Special Correspondent

The newest member of the Geyser Creek Middle School seventh-grade class is a real honey—a honey*bee*, that is, with the unique ability to spell.

"At first none of us believed a bee could really spell," said student Minnie O. "But Honey can!"

"All you have to do is tell Honey a word," explained classmate Shelly. "When she hears it, she starts tracing the letters in the air."

Caring for Honey is one of the class's assignments from Florence Waters. The famous designer is teaching the students by correspondence class this semester while their regular teacher, Mr. Sam N., fills in for Principal Walter Russ.

"My goal as acting principal is to improve school communication," said Mr. N. "Communication is the key to good relationships. I want everyone to work on their relationships this year."

Students study Honey, the spelling bee.

Mr. N. vows to improve school communication.

∽ *Bee Sweet!* ∽

In an attempt to foster kindness and good manners, the *Gazette* is encouraging people who've experienced unusual acts of sweetness to share their stories.

Thanks to everyone for making me feel so welcome here at Geyser Creek Middle School. Please forgive me if I don't respond to your greetings. I'm deaf.
—Sugar Kube

Send your Bee Sweet stories to:
The *Gazette*, Geyser Creek, Mo.

Local Stylist Wins Hairdo Contest

Pearl has a lot to do to prepare for Do Bee.

Pearl O. Ster, owner of The Fountainhead Salon, took top honors at last night's Hair's the Thing competition in St. Louis.

Ster is now eligible to compete in the National Do Bee on December 31. Contestants in the Do Bee must travel to New York City and create an original hairdo on a model of their choice.

"The National Do Bee is a big to-do, folks," Ster said. "I gotta come up with a hairdo that's flat-out fantabulous."

ℭafe ℱlorence

Everyone in Geyser Creek is invited to a
Baby Shower for Goldie and Sam
Tomorrow afternoon
Hosted by Angel Fisch and Chef Angelo

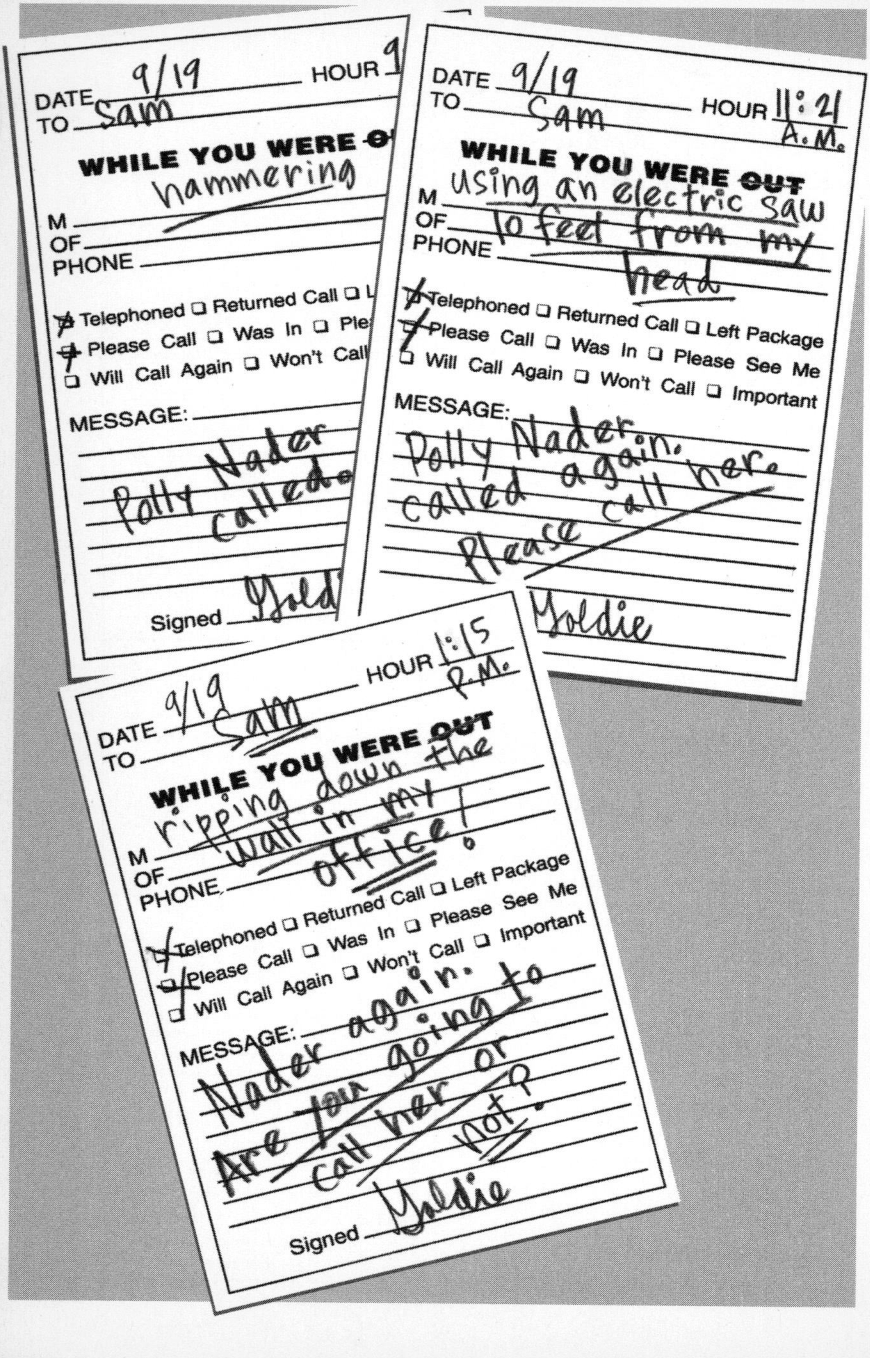
DATE 9/19 HOUR 9
TO Sam
WHILE YOU WERE ~~OUT~~ hammering
M
OF
PHONE
☑ Telephoned ☐ Returned Call ☐ L
☑ Please Call ☐ Was In ☐ Ple
☐ Will Call Again ☐ Won't Call
MESSAGE: Polly Nader called.
Signed Gold

DATE 9/19
TO Sam HOUR 11:21 A.M.
WHILE YOU WERE ~~OUT~~ using an electric saw 10 feet from my head
M
OF
PHONE
☑ Telephoned ☐ Returned Call ☐ Left Package
☑ Please Call ☐ Was In ☐ Please See Me
☐ Will Call Again ☐ Won't Call ☐ Important
MESSAGE: Polly Nader called again. Please call here
Goldie

DATE 9/19 HOUR 1:15 P.M.
TO Sam
WHILE YOU WERE ~~OUT~~ ripping down the wall in my office!
M
OF
PHONE
☑ Telephoned ☐ Returned Call ☐ Left Package
☑ Please Call ☐ Was In ☐ Please See Me
☐ Will Call Again ☐ Won't Call ☐ Important
MESSAGE: Nader again. Are you going to call her or not?
Signed Goldie

GEYSER CREEK MIDDLE SCHOOL
Geyser Creek, Missouri

Goldie Fisch-N.
School Secretary

September 19

Sam,

It's impossible to talk with all the noise in here, so I thought I'd write you a note.

The mail arrived an hour ago. I sorted and delivered it, which I don't mind doing. But usually Wally does the mail sorting.

I also answered your phone three times today. Polly Nader from Springfield Middle School wants to talk to you. (Please note: Wally always answered his own phone.)

When do you think your construction project will be finished?

Goldie

P.S. I still don't understand why you weren't at the baby shower yesterday. I told you about it at least ten times. Do you know how much work my sister and Angelo put into planning that?

September 19

Goldie,

I'm sorry for the noise—and for missing those phone calls. And I'm especially sorry about the baby shower. I'm sure you told me. I just don't remember hearing anything about it. I've got a lot on my mind these days. But that's no excuse. I really am sorry.

Honey, I'm knocking down the wall between our offices because I want to improve communication in the school. Plus, I want to be able to see you and talk with you during the day. Okay?

Please don't be mad at me.

Love,

Sam

GEYSER CREEK MIDDLE SCHOOL
Geyser Creek, Missouri

Goldie Fisch-N.
School Secretary

September 19

Sam,

I'm not mad. I was just disappointed—especially when I saw how happy Angel and Angelo looked at the shower yesterday. Did you know their baby is due the same week as ours?

I envy how Angel and Angelo still go on dates. You and I haven't been on a date since we got married.

I know you have a lot on your plate with this new job. I just want you to remember that I've also got a lot on my plate. Make that *plates*, because I'm eating for two these days.

I'm leaving for a doctor's appointment. See you tonight.

Love,

Goldie

P.S. Don't forget to call Polly Nader. She just called again!

September 19

Goldie,

Thanks, sweetheart. I'll make it up to you. I'm going to plan the perfect date for us.

I'm calling Polly Nader right now. I wonder what on earth she wants—besides the HIVE Prize.

Love,

Sam

BEE Sharp   **BEE Smart**   **BEE Successful**

September 19

Mr. Sam N.
Acting Principal
Geyser Creek Middle School
Geyser Creek, Missouri

Dear Mr. N.,

Good grief! I got tired of repeating myself on the
phone, so I'll just put this in a letter.

We would like to invite your seventh-grade class to this
year's Show-Me Spelling Bee.

Enclosed please find an invitation. Tell your seventh-
grade students to respond directly to my seventh-grade
students.

Happy spelling!

Mrs. Polly Nader

Mrs. Polly Nader

The **Seventh Graders** *at*
Springfield Middle School

**(who just happen to be the
Reigning Champions of the Show-Me Spelling Bee,
thanks to their dedicated coach and wonderful teacher,
MRS. POLLY NADER)**

Cordially Invite
Your Class
to the

SHOW-ME SPELLING BEE

on
Monday, December 5
at
7:00 P.M.

Springfield Middle School

RSVP to the Yellow Jackets
(That's our team name.)

Springfield Middle School
Springfield, Missouri

September 21

The Yellow Jackets
Mrs. Polly Nader's Seventh-Grade Class
Springfield Middle School
Springfield, Missouri

Dear Yellow Jackets,

We accept your invitation to the Show-Me Spelling Bee.

See you on December 5.

Sincerely,

Tad

Shelly   Lily   Paddy   Gil   Minnie O.

P.S. Hope it's okay for us to enter a real bee in the spelling bee.

THE YELLOW JACKETS

Mrs. Polly Nader's Seventh Grade Class
Springfield Middul School
Springfield, Misery

Septembur 23

The Seventh Grade Corruspondunce Class
Geyser Creak Middul School
Geyser Creak, Misery

DEAR LOOZERS-2-BE,

GLAD TO HERE YOUR GOING TO AHTEND THIS YEARS
SHOW-ME SPELLING BEE.

But what do you meen your enturing a spelling
bee in the spelling bee? You don't meen the
inseckt, dew you?

Right back E-meatyetly with you're
ectsplinayshun.

Sin-sara-lee,

Maureen ("Moe") Skitto

P. Daddy Longlegs

HORACE FLY

24

Seventh-Grade Correspondence Class
Geyser Creek Middle School
Geyser Creek, Missouri

September 26

The Yellow Jackets
Mrs. Polly Nader's Seventh-Grade Class
Springfield Middle School
Springfield, Missouri

Dear Yellow Jackets,

Yes, we mean the insect. Our friend Florence Waters sent us Honey, a bee that can spell every word in the *Oxford English Dictionary*.

Florence is our substitute teacher this semester. She's teaching our class by correspondence course.

Maybe you've heard of Florence? She's a famous fountain designer who lives in California. She uses only beeswax candles in her house.

She's teaching us cool things, like how ancient Egyptians used honey to embalm bodies.

Please let us know if we can enter Honey in the Show-Me Spelling Bee.

Speaking of which, how in the world did you win last year's competition?

Sincerely,

Tad   Gil   Lily   Paddy   Shelly

Minnie O.

25

THE YELLOW JACKETS

Mrs. Polly Nader's Seventh Grade Class
Springfield Middul School
Springfield, Misery

Septembur 28

The Seventh Grade Corruspondunce Class
Geyser Creak Middul School
Geyser Creak, Misery

Dear Loozers-2-Be,

You guys must be nutz.

You can't enter a reel bee in the Show-Me Spelling Bee.
It has to bee a purrson. Well, we think thats the rewel
ennyway. We'll ask Mrs. Nader. She nose all the
regyuleayshuns.

Fur your infurmayshun, we one last years Show-Me
Spelling Bee becaws we had Mrs. Polly Nader fur our
teechur. She's our teechur this year two.

Sin-sara-lee,

Maureen ("Moe") Skitto

P. Daddy Longlegs

Horace Fly

P.S. You rote "speaking of which." Is Florence Waters a
WHICH? Thats reelie creepie.

26

Seventh-Grade Correspondence Class
Geyser Creek Middle School
Geyser Creek, Missouri

September 30

The Yellow Jackets
Mrs. Polly Nader's Seventh-Grade Class
Springfield Middle School
Springfield, Missouri

Dear Yellow Jackets,

Yes. Florence is teaching our class by writing letters to us, *which* makes learning fun.

Tad
Gil
Minnie O.
Lily
Paddy
Shelly

THE YELLOW JACKETS

Mrs. Polly Nader's Seventh Grade Class
Springfield Middul School
Springfield, Misery

Ocktoeburr 3

MRS. NADER,

THE SEVINTH GRADIRS AT GEYSER CREAK MIDDUL SCHOOL WANT TO ENTUR A REEL BEE IN THE SHOW-ME SPELLING BEE. IZZAT LEGUL?

They got the bee from there subsdatoot teechur. She's a laydee named Florence Waters who lives in Californya and duzn't have reel lites—only canduls.

She soundz spookie. But they sed she makes lurning fun.

HORACE FLY

P. Daddy Longlegs

Maureen ("Moe") Skitto

TODAY'S DATE: OCTOBER 3

YOU DOPES!

FLORENCE WATERS IS A WORLD-FAMOUS FOUNTAIN DESIGNER. THOSE BRATS AT GEYSER CREEK MIDDLE SCHOOL ADORE HER. IF SHE'S TEACHING, I'M IN TROUBLE. BIG TROUBLE. I NEED TO RETHINK THE PLAN.

OH WAIT. I JUST THOUGHT OF SOMETHING.

TODAY'S ASSIGNMENT: SPEND THE REST OF THE DAY COPYING THOSE LETTERS I WROTE FOR YOU ABOUT WHY I SHOULD WIN THE HIVE PRIZE. AND KEEP YOUR STUPID TRAPS SHUT. IF I'VE TOLD YOU ONCE, I'VE TOLD YOU A MILLION TIMES: THERE'S NOTHING <u>FUN</u> ABOUT LEARNING.

MRS. NADER

BEE Sharp

BEE Smart

BEE Successful

DO NOT TOUCH!

BEE Sharp   **BEE Smart**   **BEE Successful**

October 3

Ms. Melissa Spelt
Executive Director
Missouri Department of Education
Jefferson City, Missouri

Dear Ms. Spelt,

I know how busy you must be, overseeing the public education system for the entire state *and* judging the HIVE Prize competition. But I'm writing to express my concern about a very troubling matter.

It seems that the seventh-grade class at Geyser Creek Middle School is being taught by a substitute teacher who isn't even in the classroom. She's in California! She's "teaching" the children by sending their assignments by letter.

Furthermore, this "teacher" has sent the children a trick bee named Honey that uses its little body to spell words.

I hope you agree that this spelling bee has no business participating in the Show-Me Spelling Bee. Bees can be very dangerous. I for one am highly sensitive to their venom.

I also hope you will find a way to get a *real* substitute teacher in the Geyser Creek Middle School seventh-grade classroom, preferably a retired army sergeant or a prison warden. It need not be someone the children especially *like*, as education must not be confused with entertainment.

Yours in good old-fashioned teaching,

Mrs. Polly Nader

Mrs. Polly Nader

P.S. As a courtesy to my fellow teachers working in the classroom trenches, may I kindly suggest that you disregard any HIVE Prize letters of recommendation for Florence Waters? That's the name of this so-called substitute teacher.

October 5

Mrs. Polly Nader
Seventh-Grade Teacher
Springfield Middle School
Springfield, Missouri

Mrs. Nader:

I appreciate your concern for the students at Geyser
Creek Middle School. But under Missouri law, properly
credentialed out-of-state residents are allowed to serve
as substitute teachers.

Also, effective this year, correspondence courses are
allowed in Missouri middle schools. As such, Florence
Waters is eligible for the HIVE Prize. Any letters of
recommendation written by students and colleagues on
behalf of Ms. Waters will be accepted and considered.

I am still reviewing the other matter of Honey, the
spelling bee.

Sincerely,

Melissa Spelt

Melissa Spelt

★ THE GEYSER CREEK GAZETTE ★

Our motto: "We have a nose for news!"

Thursday, October 6   **Early Edition**   **50 cents**

Can a Bee Be in a Bee?
(We'll C!)

By Tad Poll, Special Correspondent

Can a honeybee that spells words by tracing the letters in the air with its tiny body compete in a spelling bee?

That's what the seventh graders at Geyser Creek Middle School want to know.

"We see no reason why Honey can't represent us in the Show-Me Spelling Bee," said Lily.

The seventh-grade class at Springfield Middle School strenuously disagrees.

"Only seventh-grade *people* can compete in the Show-Me Spelling Bee," said Horace Fly in a telephone interview. "Besides, we didn't invite Honey. You have to be invited to come to the Show-Me Spelling Bee."

The seventh graders at Geyser Creek Middle School contend that the Yellow Jackets invited their entire class.

"And Honey is a member of our class," said Paddy.

Mrs. Polly Nader, teacher and coach of the Yellow Jackets, said the rules are unclear as to whether an insect can participate in the spelling competition.

"I've forwarded the question to Ms. Spelt, executive director of the Missouri Department of Education," said Nader. "She's reviewing the matter."

The Yellow Jackets say Honey was not invited to the Show-Me Spelling Bee.

GCMS seventh graders say their bee should be eligible for the bee.

Polly Nader: Teaching to the Test?

Although most students and teachers dread the arrival of the Basic Education Evaluation (BEE), at least one teacher looks forward to the annual event.

"I enjoy watching my students succeed," said Polly Nader, seventh-grade teacher at Springfield Middle School.

Last year Nader's students scored highest in the state on the BEEs, leading some educators to speculate that Nader helps her students by revealing to them in advance what material will be on the BEE.

Nader flatly denies the allegation.

"How could I teach to the test?" Nader asked. "I don't even know what's going to be on the BEEs until the day they arrive. And I never say a word to the students on the day of the test. Not a single word."

Nader's lips are sealed on test day.

Goldie Won't Do for Do-Bee Do

Pearl O. Ster repeated her plea yesterday regarding the National Do Bee.

"I need hair models, folks," Ster stated. "I'm asking everyone to stop by my salon so I can practice new hairdos."

Ster is preparing to compete in the National Do Bee on December 31. Contestants must bring a hair model to New York City and create an original hairstyle onstage.

"I haven't found my model yet or decided what hairdo to do," stressed Ster.

Geyser Creek Middle School secretary Goldie Fisch-N. volunteered.

"But Goldie wouldn't do for a Do-Bee due to her due date and the fact that she'd be in deep doo-doo with her doctor if she did," Ster said.

Pearl says Goldie's a no-go for hair show.

Sam N.
Acting Principal
Geyser Creek Middle School
Geyser Creek, Missouri

October 6

Hello, seventh graders.

I haven't heard any noise from your room, so I'm assuming everything's under control.

Did you see the *Gazette* today? This year's BEE sounds unusually nasty. You might want to let Florence know.

Thanks.

Mr. N.

P.S. What have you decided about the annual seventh-grade class dance? Please stop by my office and tell me your thoughts.

October 6

Florence Waters
Famous Designer and Our Favorite Teacher
Flowing Waters Fountains, Etc.
Watertown, California

Hiya, Florence!

Please cross your fingers. We're waiting to hear if Honey can represent us in the Show-Me Spelling Bee. She's our best chance of beating the Yellow Jackets!

The Yellow Jackets is the team name for the seventh-grade class at Springfield Middle School.

It's the perfect name for them because they're annoying little pests who like to bug us.

At least the Yellow Jackets are cute. I saw their picture in the paper today. We don't have any cute boys at this school.

Even Mr. N. is being sort of ugly this year. We just went down to his office to tell him our class had taken a vote and decided <u>not</u> to have a dance on New Year's Eve. But Mr. N. wouldn't even look up from his desk. Sheesh!

Anyway, Mr. N. wanted us to tell you the BEEs are going to be really nasty this year. Can you please help us get ready for them?

And do you think you could help us learn sign language? We want to know how to say <u>hi</u> and <u>thanks</u> to our new school custodian, Sugar Kube. She's deaf.

Bye for now!   Lily   Paddy

35

October 6

Ms. Florence Waters
Friend, Fountain Designer, and Substitute Teacher
Flowing Waters Fountains, Etc.
Watertown, California

Dear Florence,

I want to thank you again for sending Honey. But goodness! That little bee is going to get me in <u>big</u> trouble!

Earlier today I was talking quietly with Lily and Paddy about boys. I told them in a whisper that I really like Gil. Honey must've heard me because she started spelling with her little body:

I R-E-A-L-L-Y L-I-K-E G-I-L

Of course, Lily and Paddy were laughing their heads off, but I could've died! Luckily, Shelly was reading a book and didn't see it. If she had, she would've been so **M-A-D** at me. I know she thinks I'm trying to steal her boyfriend, but I'm not. I can't help it that I think Gil is the sweetest boy on earth—even though he won't even <u>look</u> at me.

Gosh, seventh grade is exhausting. I don't know how to act around Shelly <u>or</u> Gil. What should I do?

Love,
   Minnie O.

P.S. The BEEs are going to be really bad this year, just so you know.

October 6

Florence Waters
Our Correspondence Course Teacher
Flowing Waters Fountains, Etc.
Watertown, California

Hey, Florence.

The BEEs are supposed to be awful this year. And you know what? I don't even care. I feel like dropping out of school.

All the other girls in my class have formed a clique. They sit together and talk and giggle, and they never ask me to join them. They think because I have a boyfriend (Gil), I don't need girlfriends.

Well, they're wrong. I'd rather be friends with them than with Gil. He's not even nice to me this year. I like Tad 100 percent better, but he can't like me because he thinks I'm Gil's girlfriend.

In a way, I hope the BEEs are really, _really_ terrible and that our whole class performs horribly on them. That way, we can all go back to fifth grade and everybody can be friends again.

Sincerely,

Shelly

P.S. Oh, and get this: We're not even going to have a class dance on New Year's Eve—even though every other seventh-grade class before us got to have one. This is the worst year _ever._

October 6

Florence Waters
President
Flowing Waters Fountains, Etc.
Watertown, California

Dear Florence,

I just got back from the roof, where I was checking on the hives. I've been checking on them four times a day. I haven't seen any bees yet. But I've noticed something else.

The first time I climbed all those stairs to the roof, it made me really tired and short of breath. But now I can run up the stairs pretty fast. I think I'm starting to build muscles in my legs.

Anyway, we have the BEEs on December 6. They're going to be really, really, REALLY bad this year. I'm trying not to think about them so I won't get hives.

I'm also trying not to think about girls—or even look at them. Luckily, we voted not to have a class dance. Thank goodness. I just don't think I'm ready to start dating. I don't know how to kiss, and if I did it wrong, Shelly would just laugh at me. She's already giving me dirty looks.

I don't want to start dating till I get to high school. Or maybe college. Do you think that's okay?

Gil

October 6

The Eternally Cool Ms. Florence Waters
Teacher and Pal
Flowing Waters Fountains, Etc.
Watertown, California

Hi, Florence!

Hope everything's going great with you. It's really fun to have
you as our teacher. I thought I'd miss Mr. N. more, but he seems
really different this year.

I just saw him in the principal's office. I told him (for the third
time) that I'd like to have a class dance—if someone would just
teach me how to dance. Chef Angelo offered to show me some
steps, but he and Angel do that old-fashioned kind of dancing.
I want to learn the *new* dances.

But Mr. N. wouldn't even talk to me. He probably thinks I'm
stupid for wanting to have a New Year's Eve dance. Nobody else
in our class wants to.

Oh well. It doesn't matter. All the girls in the class like Gil,
anyway. I think he's been working out or something.

Well, that's the buzz from here—except for the dreaded BEEs.
Are you going to help us get ready for them? They're supposed
to be nasty this year.

Your friend,

Tad

Watertown, California

October 10

The Seventh-Grade Sweeties
Geyser Creek Middle School
Geyser Creek, Missouri

Dear Lily, Paddy, Minnie O., Shelly, Gil, and Tad:

I'm crossing my fingers—and my toes—that Honey can represent you in the Show-Me Spelling Bee. But I'm sure you all are queen-bee spellers!

And of course I'm going to help you prepare for the BEEs. If I didn't, what kind of friend would *I* be? In fact, I'm leaving soon to begin my BEE research. (Don't worry: I have my mail forwarded when I travel, so keep writing letters to me. Our correspondence course will continue uninterrupted.)

I've enclosed your next assignments.

I'm also enclosing more bees. Gil, gently place these bees in the hives on the school roof. Their flight pattern will be high enough so as not to bother anyone at school. These bees like late-blooming flowers, so they should be very happy collecting nectar in Geyser Creek this time of year.

Did you know that late-blooming flowers are often the nicest flowers of all? Nature has a wonderful sense of timing from which we can all learn.

Your friend,

H. F. lorence

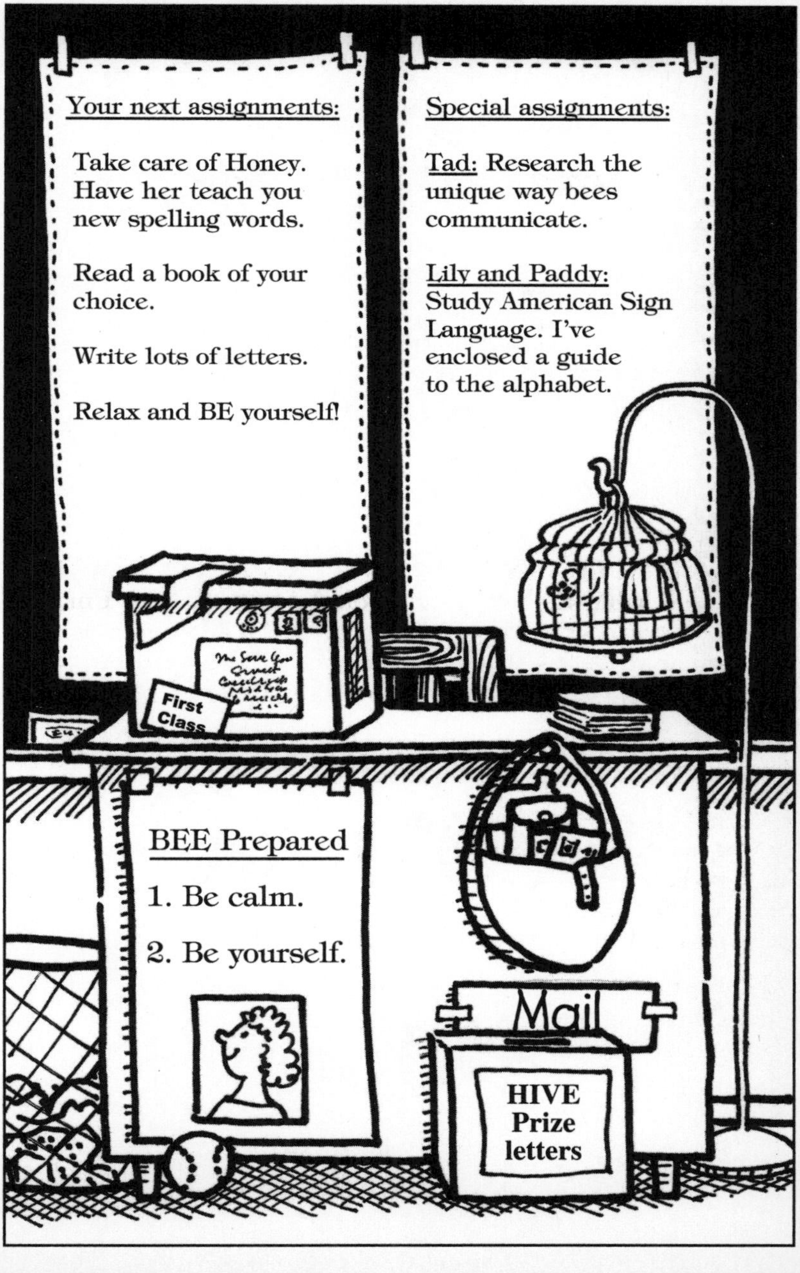
Your next assignments:
Take care of Honey. Have her teach you new spelling words.
Read a book of your choice.
Write lots of letters.
Relax and BE yourself!
Special assignments:
Tad: Research the unique way bees communicate.
Lily and Paddy: Study American Sign Language. I've enclosed a guide to the alphabet.
First Class
BEE Prepared
1. Be calm.
2. Be yourself.
Mail
HIVE Prize letters

AMERICAN SIGN LANGUAGE CHART

A

B

C

D

E

F

G

H

I

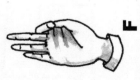
J

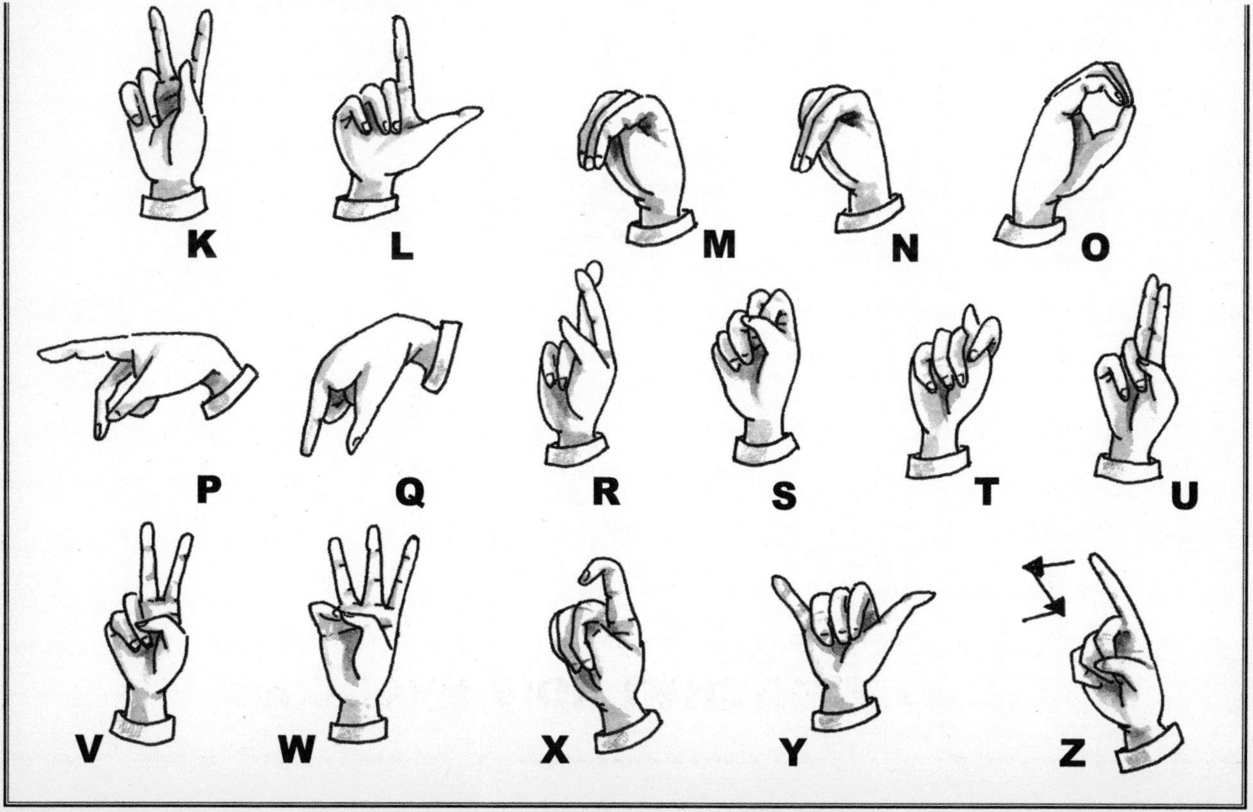
K
L
M
N
O
P
Q
R
S
T
U
V
W
X
Y
Z

How Bees Communicate

Special Assignment

By Tad Poll

Did you know that bees communicate by *dancing*?

It's true!

When a honeybee returns to the hive, the bee shares nectar with its hivemates. Then it performs a special dance to communicate the distance, direction, quality, and quantity of nearby nectar sources.

If the nectar supply is near the hive, the bee does the "round dance."

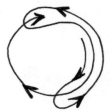

Round dance: Turn in circles alternately to the left and to the right.

If the food supply is farther away, the bee performs the "waggle dance."

flowers
40°
sun
flowers
40°
gravity

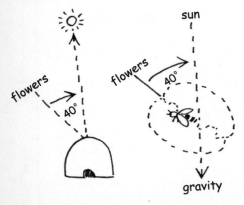

Waggle dance: Make two loops with a straight run in the middle.

Cafe Florence

Located in Geyser Creek Middle School

Angel Fisch

October 11

Hey, Goldie!

None of my beeswax, but what's up with Sam? He was just in the cafe. I said hi, but he kept walking.

Now that he's principal, does he think he's too much of a big shot to talk to his sister-in-law?

Well, you know I love you, sis. If you need to talk, holler.

Don't forget we have doctor appointments tomorrow in Springfield.

Love,

Angel

P.S. Here are some oatmeal-date cookies. We got ten cases of imported dates as a wedding gift from Angelo's aunt Angelica in Italy. I can't stand the smushy things, but Angelo loves dates. So, I just pretend to like them, too.

Angel,

Thanks for the cookies. You know I love dates—both the kind you eat *and* the kind you go on.

Sorry about Sam. He's driving me crazy, too. I don't know what to do.

Goldie

P.S. I wish Florence were here. She always has good advice. Maybe I'll write her a letter.

GEYSER CREEK MIDDLE SCHOOL
Geyser Creek, Missouri

Goldie Fisch-N.
School Secretary

October 11

Florence Waters
Friend and Personal Adviser
Flowing Waters Fountains, Etc.
Watertown, California

Dear Florence,

Do you have time to listen to a friend's problems? If so, read on.

As you know, Wally is away this semester. Sam is filling in as principal. For the first time in our lives, Sam and I are working together in the same office. The problem is, it's *not* working.

Do you remember how sweet Sam used to be? Do you recall what a good listener he was? Well, I wish I knew where *that* Sam went. As principal, Sam ignores both me and his responsibilities. Plus, he treats me like his slave. Say what you will about Principal Russ, at least he answered his own darn phone.

Meanwhile, Chef Angelo couldn't be sweeter to my sister. Every Saturday night, he and Angel go out on a date. I'm so jealous I could scream! Sam and I date *weakly*, if at all. When it comes to romance, my husband has a tin ear.

Oh gosh. I hate to be such a complainer. Let me end with some happy news: The seventh graders are nominating you for the Highly Innovative and Victorious Educator (HIVE) Prize. The winner gets $1,000,000!

In the meantime, I'm enclosing your paycheck.

Goldie

Goldie Fisch-N.

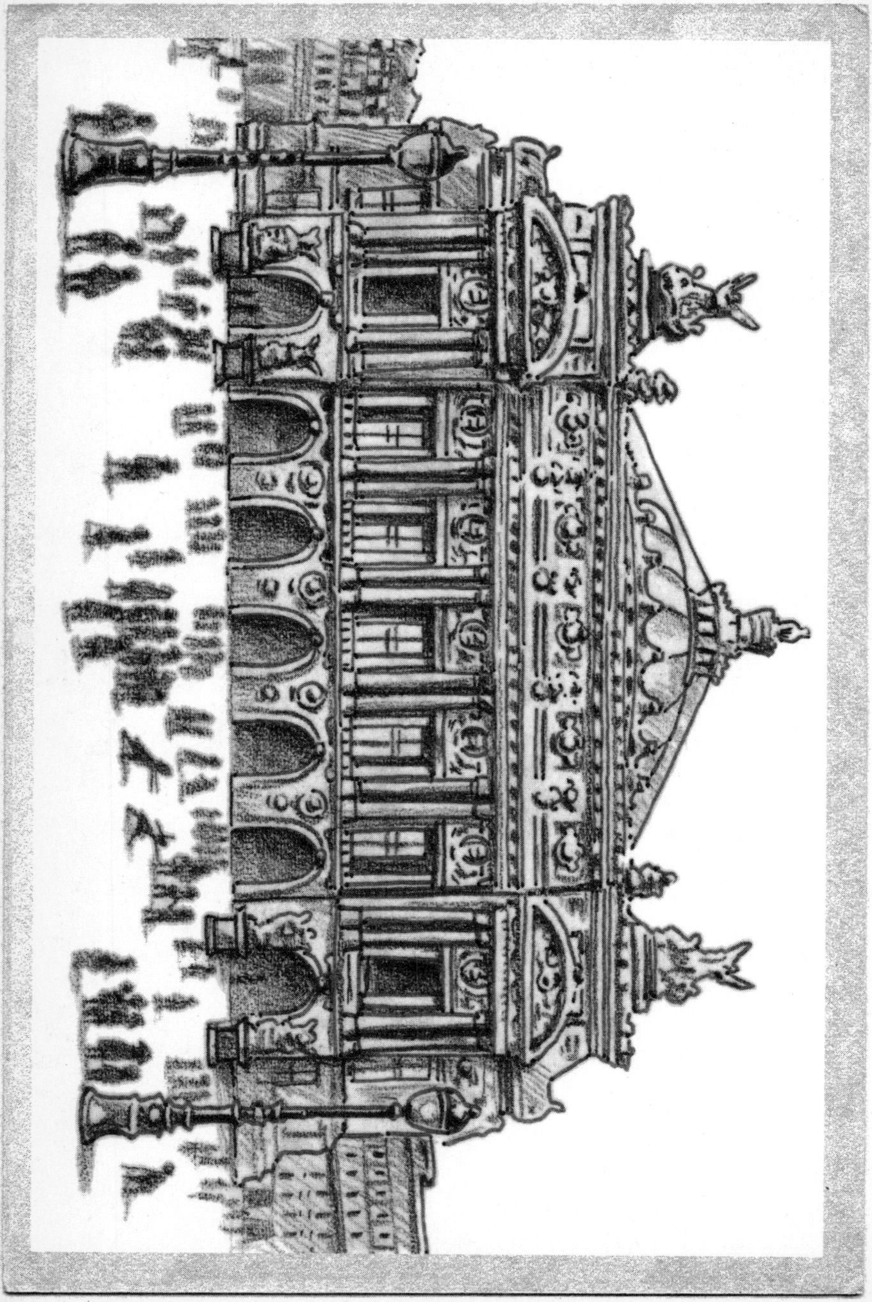

PRIORITAIRE
PRIORITY

Sam and Goldie,
You two have been best friends for as long as you've known. If you've problems, I urge you to talk and -ing to listen to really each other. I'm as busy -
Gotta run - Jim as busy - Winged the -win seventh- a-wing class for the preparade BEES. Love, Flo

Sam W. & Goldie Nach. Jr.
Denser Creek Middle
Denser Creek School
Denseroni USA 5

Goldie: No offence. Winsonni.
No offence. the
writing
P.S. to Goldie: I'drew writing
this but I drew students
suexcept away students; not
Ponhtere to job, not
Ponhtere a job. is a job.

105

Sam N.
Acting Principal
Geyser Creek Middle School
Geyser Creek, Missouri

October 18

Florence Waters
c/o Palais Garnier
Place de l'Opéra
Paris, France

Dear Florence,

So, I guess you know.

Goldie's mad at me because she thinks I'm a) not doing a good job as principal, b) ignoring her, and c) going to be a lousy father to our baby.

But it's even worse than Goldie knows. The truth is, I think I'm going deaf.

As of today, I've lost all hearing in my left ear and can hear only very loud noises in my right ear. This means I won't be able to keep my job as a teacher when Mr. Russ returns. I won't hear my child's first words. I don't even know if Goldie will want to stay married to me.

Mr. Russ told me that after spending a few months as principal, I'd find that silence was golden. I couldn't disagree more.

Sincerely,

Sam N.

P.S. Since you brought it up, dare I ask how you're preparing your class for the BEEs? The students must perform well on them in order to advance to eighth grade.

PARIS

October 20

Sam N.
Acting Principal
Geyser Creek Middle School
Geyser Creek, Missouri USA

Dear Sam,

I'm very sorry about your hearing loss, but you must make a beeline to your doctor's office to get a proper diagnosis. No ifs, ands, or buts about it. And then you have to tell Goldie.

Regarding the BEEs: Of course I want the seventh graders to perform well on those beasts, but I'm not willing to let them get hurt in the process. That's why I'm working with my favorite designer here in Paris to create special suits and helmets for the students to wear while they tackle the nasty creatures.

H. Florence

HOTEL FONTAINE

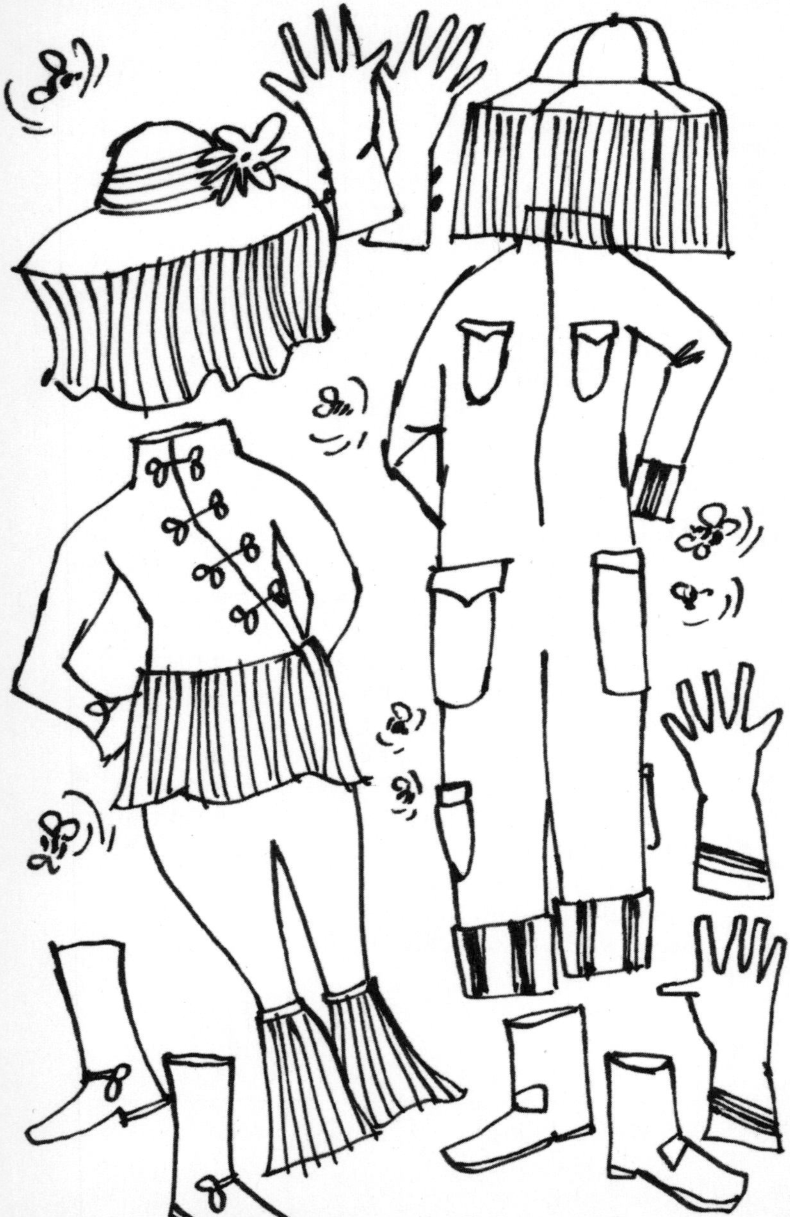

Sam N.
Acting Principal
Geyser Creek Middle School
Geyser Creek, Missouri

October 21

Florence Waters
Guest
Hotel Fontaine
Paris, France

Dear Florence,

Thanks for your concern regarding the BEEs. You're always so generous with the students. But really, I don't think designer suits are necessary. Helmets would actually be a hindrance. The students must be able to *see* the BEEs.

I know I should see a doctor about my ears. But I'm terrified of doctors—and I hate getting shots.

(Now you know what a coward I really am.)

Sincerely,

Sam N.

PARIS

October 24

Sam N.
Acting Principal
  Who's Acting Like a Big Baby
Geyser Creek Middle School
Geyser Creek, Missouri USA

Sam!

What's gotten into you?

You don't like getting shots, but you don't mind allowing giant BEEs to come into your school and torment the students?

Please see a doctor who can examine your ears *and* your brain. And then find a friend to talk to regarding your relationship with Goldie.

Betwixt, bothered, and bewildered by you,

Florence

HOTEL FONTAINE

Sam N.
Acting Principal
Geyser Creek Middle School
Geyser Creek, Missouri

CONFIDENTIAL

October 26

Chef Angelo
Cafe Florence
Geyser Creek Middle School
Geyser Creek, Missouri

Dear Angelo,

I need some advice.

Goldie and I were best friends for years before we got married in May. You and Angel knew each other for only a month. And yet, you two now seem happier than Goldie and me.

Have you figured out the secret to women? I'd appreciate any wisdom you can offer.

Thanks.

Sam N.

Cafe Florence

Located in Geyser Creek Middle School

Chef Angelo

BIG SECRETY

October 27

Sam N.
My brother-in-law and the principal for the right now
Guys "R" Creek Middle School
Guys "R" Creek, Missouri

Hello, my good friend and the almost brother-outlaw!

You are having the problem with the marriage and the job. What am I thinking about this? I will tell you right now.

Our wives, they like to talk to us. This is the wonderful thing. But if they think when they are talking to us that we are thinking about the work or the pasta or the football? This is very bad. This makes the wives mad as big angry bees. Why? Because the wives think we are not paying them the good attention. They also think we do not love them.

So this is what I say to you: If you want to be the good husband, you must have the good ears.

I must to go now. I am baking the banana bread with dates. Aunt Angelica, she send ten cases of dates for the wedding gift. To me, the dates they hurt my teeth because they are too sweet. But my Angel, she loves them, so I put them in every little thing and I pretend I so love them.

This is what we call the *sacrificio*. It is what the marriage is all about.

Chef Angelo

☆ THE GEYSER CREEK GAZETTE ☆

Our motto: "We have a nose for news!"

Saturday, October 29   **Early Edition**   **50 cents**

Spelling Bee Can't Be in Spelling Bee

By Tad Poll, Special Correspondent

Honey, the bee that can spell, cannot be in the Show-Me Spelling Bee.

"After reviewing the matter thoroughly, I have determined that eligibility in spelling bees is limited to human beings," said Melissa "Missy" Spelt, executive director of the Missouri Department of Education, at a press conference held yesterday in Jefferson City.

However, Honey can attend the Show-Me Spelling Bee on December 5.

"Honey may go as a mascot but not as a competitor," said Ms. Spelt.

The seventh graders at Geyser Creek Middle School were disappointed by the ruling.

"We think it's totally unfair," said Shelly.

Honey seconded the emotion by spelling the words *totally unfair* as the seventh-grade class cheered.

Geyser Creek Middle School Acting Principal Sam N. could not be reached for comment on the decision.

"If he thinks I'm going to answer his phone, he is W-R-O-N-G," said school secretary Goldie Fisch-N., who also happens to be Mr. N.'s wife.

Ms. Spelt announces her decision regarding the spelling bee.

Students and Honey call the ruling T-O-T-A-L-L-Y U-N-F-A-I-R.

BEE Czar Issues Bizarre Warning

B. B. King says students should prepare for very unusual BEEs.

Benny Bob "B. B." King, director of the Basic Education Evaluation (BEE), issued a warning yesterday to Missouri middle school students and teachers.

"This year's BEE will be like no other BEE you've ever seen," said King, who urged teachers to make an extra effort to adequately prepare students for the BEEs, which will be given on December 6.

"But keep in mind that teachers may not assist students in any way on the day of the BEEs," said King.

King reminded middle school students that the BEEs become part of their permanent record and follow them to college. He also noted the new rule for seventh graders.

"Any seventh grader who fails the BEE will be personally escorted back to fifth grade," said King. "That's why we call them the BEEs—because they can really sting."

Florence Waters: Substitute Teaching for Free

By Tad Poll, Special Correspondent

Leave it to Florence Waters to turn down a paycheck.

The world-famous fountain designer has refused to accept payment for teaching the seventh-grade class at Geyser Creek Middle School by correspondence course.

"Isn't that just like Florence?" said Minnie O. "We think she's the greatest."

Not surprisingly, the class is writing letters of recommendation for Waters to the Missouri Department of Education, making her eligible for the Highly Innovative and Victorious Educator (HIVE) Prize.

In addition to writing letters, the students are caring for bees, reading, learning new spelling words and studying American Sign Language.

Office Suite Turns Sour
Sweeties nearly split over suite renovation

Are Sam N. and Goldie Fisch-N. too close for comfort?

Sam N. has made a mess of his first seven weeks as acting principal of Geyser Creek Middle School. Literally.

The trouble began when he started tearing down the wall that separates his office from that of school secretary Goldie Fisch-N.

"I thought it would open up the lines of communication," said Mr. N., who married Fisch in May.

Instead, the construction project seems to be driving the two apart—and at the worst possible time. Sam and Goldie are expecting their first child in February.

Seventh graders nominate Waters for HIVE Prize.

October 31

Ms. Melissa Spelt
Executive Director
Missouri Department of Education
Jefferson City, Missouri

Dear Ms. Spelt,

Thank you for your prudent ruling on Honey, the spelling bee. And I'm sorry to bother you again, but I simply cannot stand by and watch an entire class of children suffer at the hands of a substitute teacher.

Yes, I am referring to Florence Waters. I will enclose a recent edition of the *Geyser Creek Gazette*. Do you see how this woman is practically *demanding* that her students nominate her for the HIVE Prize? Do you see how she is *manipulating* their affections by turning down a paycheck? What teacher wouldn't teach for free? I know I would.

But Florence Waters lives out of state—in California, for heaven's sake! And you know what *those* people are like. Can you imagine what a slap in the face it would be to card-carrying Missouri teachers if this *interloper* won the HIVE Prize?

I hope you'll reconsider your decision to allow Florence Waters to continue substitute teaching at Geyser Creek Middle School.

Yours in learning,

Mrs. Polly Nader

Mrs. Polly Nader

59

November 2

Mrs. Polly Nader
Seventh-Grade Teacher
Springfield Middle School
Springfield, Missouri

Mrs. Nader:

Any employee working for a Missouri school has the
right to turn down a paycheck. I think your concerns
about Ms. Waters are ill founded.

Sincerely,

Melissa Spelt

Melissa Spelt

P.S. I wouldn't worry, Mrs. Nader. Your students are
the reigning champs of both the BEEs and the Show-Me
Spelling Bee. Plus, I've already received 14,565 letters of
recommendation from them on your behalf. The HIVE
Prize is practically yours already.

November 2

Ms. Florence Waters
Designer, Teacher, Company President
Flowing Waters Fountains, Etc.
Watertown, California

Hey, Florence.

Crummy news here. We can't enter Honey in the Show-Me Spelling Bee. All we can do is take her to Springfield with us as our mascot.

But never mind that. I can't believe bees *dance*! I did some research on it for my special assignment. Then I started studying the bees on the school roof. It's so cool how they do these funny dances—making loops and turns—to show the other bees in the hive where the best flowers are for nectar. I'm going to try to learn those bee dances myself.

Hope you're doing okay. I am, but that will change when the BEEs arrive in December.

Your pal,

Tad Poll

Seventh-Grade Correspondence Class
Geyser Creek Middle School
Geyser Creek, Missouri

November 2

Florence Waters
My Teacher and Friend
Flowing Waters Fountains, Etc.
Watertown, California

Dear Florence,

I hope you didn't think I was complaining when I wrote you in my last letter about how Honey had spelled out my feelings for Gil.

She really is a sweet little bee. She's helping us train for the Show-Me Spelling Bee. Someone in the class will say a word, and we all try to spell it in our notebooks. Then, Honey spells it in front of the class and we can check our work. It's fun!

Florence, are you going to help us get ready for the BEEs? We have to take them the day after the Show-Me Spelling Bee. I don't want to tell you how to teach, but we should probably start preparing for the BEEs now. They're only a month away. Did you know the BEEs follow us to college?

Sincerely,

Minnie O.

P.S. Shelly must've figured out that I like Gil because today she moved her desk away from mine. I feel terrible because Shelly used to be one of my best friends. I can't help it that I like her boyfriend. It's not like I want to marry him or anything. I just want to be his friend. But he won't even look at me.

62

November 2

Florence Waters
President
Flowing Waters Fountains, Etc.
Watertown, California

Hi, Florence.

I finally moved my desk away from Gil, who won't give me the time of day. I'm now sitting next to Tad. At least he'll talk to me—unlike the girls in the class and Gil.

Even Mr. N. gave me the cold shoulder today. I said hey to him in the hallway, but he just walked by without saying hello.

I know if you were here, you'd tell me not to take all this so personally. But it's hard not to. At least the stupid New Year's Eve class dance is canceled. Can you imagine going on a date with a boy who won't even talk to you?

Well, thanks for listening to my problems, Florence. I really appreciate it. You're the best friend I have this year.

Shelly

November 2

Florence Waters
Substitute Teacher
Flowing Waters Fountains, Etc.
Watertown, California

Dear Florence,

You'd be surprised how fast I can run up to the roof now. I take the steps two by two, which cuts my time in half. I am definitely getting stronger and less skinny.

I added some arm weights, too. Well, not *real* weights. But the *Oxford English Dictionary* is pretty heavy. And I found another big book titled *The Complete Works of William Shakespeare*. So now I'm carrying those on my roof runs.

Yesterday when I got up to the roof, I opened the Shakespeare book and started reading *Hamlet*. It's sorta violent and some of the language is pretty racy—once you figure out what they're saying. I know I should be preparing for the Show-Me Spelling Bee and the BEEs, but I might keep reading about this Hamlet guy. It's pretty good.

One bad thing: I must not have worn enough deodorant today because after I got back from my last run to the roof, Shelly moved her desk away from mine. When she did, Minnie O. almost started crying. That's how much everyone hates sitting by me.

Oh well. At least they'll be happy when I get sent back to fifth grade. That's what will happen when I flunk the BEEs.

Gil

November 2

Florence Waters
The World's Best Substitute Teacher
Flowing Waters Fountains, Etc.
Watertown, California

Dear Florence,

Did you hear that Honey can't represent us in the Show-Me Spelling Bee? She was the best chance we had to beat the Yellow Jackets at Springfield Middle School.

The Yellow Jackets are sorta jerks, but the boys on that team are really cute! Here's a question for you, Florence: Do you think it's okay to like cute boys—even if they're dimwits and not very nice?

And even if they can't write a decent letter? You should see the letters the Yellow Jackets sent our class. Their handwriting is terrible, and they can't spell to save their L-I-V-E-S. Is it mean of us to hold their bad spelling against them?

Please write back in a _private_ letter. We don't want the other girls to know we like the enemy. And we certainly don't want Gil and Tad to know we don't think they're cute.

But the truth is, if those Yellow Jackets were in our class, we'd <u>definitely</u> ask them to be our boyfriends.

Lily   Paddy

P.S. Thanks for sending us the guide to American Sign Language!

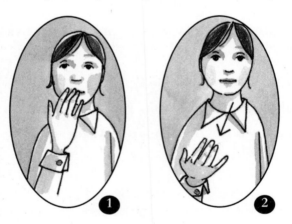

This is how you sign _thank you_.

La Araña
Valencia, Spain

November 5

CORREO AÉREO
RÁPIDO

The Stupendous Seventh Graders at
Geyser Creek Middle School
Geyser Creek, Missouri USA

Dear Studious Students,

Thank you for the newsy letters. They were forwarded to me
here in Spain, where I'm continuing my research.

I cannot believe those dastardly BEEs follow you to college.
The relentless little devils! Don't worry. I'm working night
and day to prepare you for those strange creatures.

I'm camping at La Araña, the Cave of the Spider. Nomadic
hunters and gatherers met here more than 8,000 years ago.
Back then, small groups of extended families traveled with
the seasons. Occasionally, the people took shelter in caves
like this, where they could rest.

Black soot on the low ceiling near the entrance of the cave
suggests the hunters lit fires to cook their meals and to stay

warm. They also painted scenes on the cave walls like this:

Can you guess what it is? A honey hunt!

The artist used a cavity in the wall to depict a bee nest. See the honey hunter climbing a rope ladder while bees gather to attack him?

Early hunters had to steal honey from the nests of bees, which were often found in trees. Even now, honey collecting is sometimes called robbing the bees because that's what we modern beekeepers do. We steal bees' honey for our own enjoyment. That's why it's important to be nice to bees.

In summary, class, please understand that people have been hunting for honey for thousands of years. Honey hunting is completely natural, though it is undeniably dangerous. You must exercise caution when hunting for your honey so as not to injure yourself or your fellow honey hunters. Done properly, finding your own honey can be very sweet and rewarding.

(I hope I'm being clear. I *do* remember how complicated seventh-grade relationships can be.)

Your friend, *Florence*

P.S. Oops! Almost forgot. Assignment enclosed.

P.P.S. So sorry to hear the news about Honey. But surely she'll enjoy the trip to Springfield. So should you.

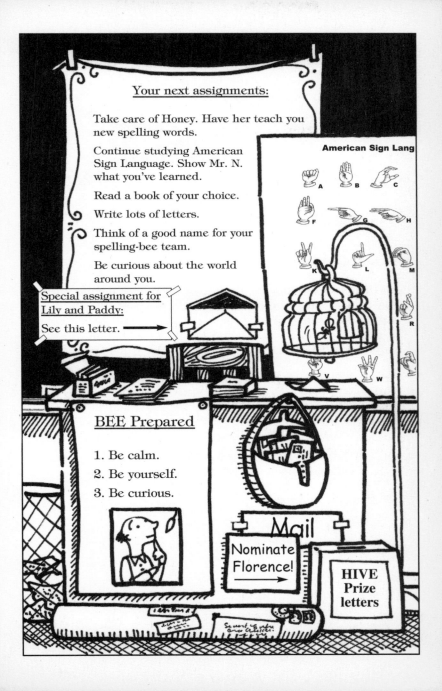

Your next assignments:

Take care of Honey. Have her teach you new spelling words.

Continue studying American Sign Language. Show Mr. N. what you've learned.

Read a book of your choice.

Write lots of letters.

Think of a good name for your spelling-bee team.

Be curious about the world around you.

Special assignment for Lily and Paddy:

See this letter. ➝

American Sign Lang

BEE Prepared

1. Be calm.
2. Be yourself.
3. Be curious.

Mail

Nominate Florence! ➝

HIVE Prize letters

La Araña
Valencia, Spain

November 5

Lily and Paddy
Seventh-Grade Correspondence Class
Geyser Creek Middle School
Geyser Creek, Missouri USA

Dear Lily and Paddy,

Regarding your question as to whether it's advisable to like boys who aren't very nice and can't spell, but who are cute: *Hmmmmm . . .*

I agree that spelling is important. But goodness, anyone can learn to spell. I've always valued rarer qualities, like honesty, kindness, and a sense of humor.

When it comes to boys, the question is not if they can spell but if they put a spell on *you.* Do they? Just by being cute? To my mind, cute is as cute *does.*

Okay, now here's a question for you: How in the world do those cute boys who can't spell win spelling bees? Be *curious,* girls!

Yours in honey hunting,

Florence

November 7

Florence Waters
Teacher, Friend, Inspiration
c/o Cave of the Spider
Valencia, Spain

Dear Florence,

How do those cute Yellow Jackets at Springfield Middle School plan to win the Show-Me Spelling Bee? There was only one way to find out.

We hitched a ride to Springfield with Goldie and Angel today so we could spy on the Yellow Jackets. While Goldie and Angel went to their doctor appointments, we camped outside Springfield Middle School.

Unfortunately, Mrs. Nader's room is on the second floor. So we're going back tomorrow with a rope ladder—just like the honey hunter used in the Cave of the Spider.

In a way it's perfect because Paddy and I <u>are</u> both hunting for a honey. (Florence, we understood your letter! Hee-hee!)

Full report to follow. Wish us luck!   Lily   paddy

SPRINGFIELD POLICE REPORT

Description of Incident

Call received at 2:10 P.M. from Polly Nader at Springfield Middle School.

Officer sent to the scene found two girls, Lily and Paddy, on a rope ladder, looking in windows of Nader's seventh-grade classroom.

Lily and Paddy are students at Geyser Creek Middle School. Say they took the bus to Springfield and were simply doing their homework.

Nader's version of events: "The little brats were snooping on us!"

Warning given to girls and parents called. No further action taken.

This concludes report by:

Millie Peed

Officer Millie Peed

November 8

☆THE GEYSER CREEK GAZETTE☆

Our motto: "We have a nose for news!"

Wednesday, November 9   **Early Edition**   **50 cents**

Yellow Jackets' Coach Mad as a Hornet

By Tad Poll, Special Correspondent

Two seventh-grade students from Geyser Creek Middle School were caught yesterday peeking in the windows at Springfield Middle School.

"We were just doing our homework," said Paddy.

"Oh, don't give me that!" snapped seventh-grade teacher Polly Nader. "What kind of crackpot teacher would instruct her students to be truants and peeping tomboys?"

Lily and Paddy defended their substitute teacher, Florence Waters.

"Florence is a wonderful teacher," said Lily. "She encourages us to be curious about the world around us."

"That's right," added Paddy. "And we're especially curious about how the Yellow Jackets are training for the Show-Me Spelling Bee. They're not very good spellers, judging from the letters they've sent us."

"But we don't hold that against them," said Lily. "Florence says that when it comes to boys, their spelling doesn't matter as much as whether they put a spell on you."

Photo by Lily

Polly Nader trains her Yellow Jackets for upcoming spelling bee.

Nader tells police that Lily and Paddy are "peeping tomboys."

Pearl Rejects Angelo and Angel as Hair Models for Do Bee

Pearl says Angelo's hair is too thin and Angel is too thick.

Thanks but no thanks.

That's what Pearl O. Ster told Chef Angelo and Angel Fisch last night after they both volunteered as hair models.

"Don't tell him I said this," stated Ster, "but Angelo's bald as an eagle. And Angel's belly's getting so big, I can't even reach her bangs."

Ster repeated her request for all Geyser Creek residents to visit her beauty shop so she can practice new hairstyles and select a model for the National Do Bee in New York City on December 31.

"Come on, folks," urged Ster. "I've just gotta come up with a good do for the Do Bee."

Acting Principal Acting Strange

By Tad Poll, Special Correspondent

Ask anyone who's been to the principal's office at Geyser Creek Middle School: Acting Principal Sam N. is acting weird.

Speaking on the condition of anonymity, students and coworkers agree that the former teacher has not had an easy time adjusting to life as principal.

"It's like Mr. N.'s forgotten how to interact with students," said one seventh grader.

"He's certainly forgotten how to treat his wife," said an office worker.

When asked by this reporter to explain his recent behavior, Mr. N. said simply: "Huh? What? Did you say something to me?"

Sam N. appears deaf to criticism.

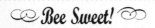

Thanks to Lily and Paddy for giving me an exclusive interview about their run-in with Mrs. Nader. You girls rock!

—Tad Poll

Have you experienced an unusual act of sweetness?
If so, we want to know about it.
Send your Bee Sweet stories to:
The *Gazette*, Geyser Creek, Mo.

A MEMO FROM MRS. POLLY NADER

BEE Sharp   **BEE Smart**   **BEE Successful**

To: The Yellow Jackets
Fr: Me
Re: Your BEEhavior
Date: November 9

You stupid monkeys!

You've been writing letters to the students at Geyser Creek Middle School? If I lose the HIVE Prize because of you cretins, there'll be big T-R-O-U-B-L-E.

I've been planning this since the day I started teaching twenty-four miserable years ago. If you think I'm going to let a bunch of DUMB PIP-SQUEAKS LIKE YOU ruin it for me now, you've got another thought coming.

Behave and pay attention to the task at hand. You wouldn't want to have to change your name from the Yellow Jackets to the *Straight*jackets, would you?

THE YELLOW JACKETS

Mrs. Polly Nader's Seventh Grade Class
Springfield Middul School
Springfield, Misery

KNOWVEMBUR 9

Mrs. Nader,

Sorry. Frum now on, we'll bee good.

We no were in good hands (ha-ha) with you.

Hey, if you win, do we still get sum of the HIVE prize muney?

P. Daddy Longlegs

Maureen ("Moe") Skitto

HORACE FLY

P.S. DID YOU NO FLORENCE WATERS IS A WHICH? THAT'S WHAT THE GUYSER CREAK 7TH GRADURS ROTE US. SHE USES ONLY BEESWAX CANDULS IN HER HOWSE. AND SHE'S TEECHING THERE CORRUSPONDUNCE CLASS HOW TO EMBALM DEAD BODYS.

A MEMO FROM MRS. POLLY NADER

BEE Sharp　　　　**BEE Smart**　　　　**BEE Successful**

To:　　The Yellow Jackets
Fr:　　Me
Re:　　Your BEEhavior
Date:　November 9

How many times do I have to explain this to you nitwits? If I win the HIVE Prize, you get 10 percent of the money.

And what do you mean Florence Waters is a which? Do you mean a *witch*? Don't be ridiculous.

Oh wait. WAIT. This is perfect. This is wonderful! This might just work.

You brats are so stupid, you're brilliant. Ha-ha! Now strap on your muzzles and copy those letters I wrote for you—word for word, letter for letter—and mail them to that Spelt broad in Jefferson City.

And for pity's sake, don't leave a bunch of incriminating notes lying around that could ruin *everything*.

THIS IS AN URGENT FAX

To: Melissa "Missy" Spelt
Fr: Mrs. Polly Nader
Re: Florence Waters

Ms. Spelt,

Forgive me for bothering you again. Forgive me for worrying about students other than my own. Forgive me for trying to protect the reputation of teachers everywhere.

But did you know that the California woman currently working as an unpaid substitute teacher for the seventh-grade class at Geyser Creek Middle School is a witch?

That's right. Florence Waters is a WITCH!

She lights her house with only beeswax candles. She sends her students a magical bee that can spell. And now she's encouraging the children to cast SPELLS *and* embalm one another—during class time!

Ms. Spelt, I am only reporting what her students have told me and others. Please, please, please, if you care about children, *do* something about Florence Waters NOW.

Yours in the name of educators everywhere,

Mrs. Polly Nader

MELISSA "MISSY" SPELT
EXECUTIVE DIRECTOR
MISSOURI DEPARTMENT OF EDUCATION
JEFFERSON CITY, MISSOURI

THIS IS AN URGENT RESPONSE
TO YOUR URGENT FAX

Mrs. Nader:

Why didn't you tell me this in the first place?

I am on the case.

Thank you for your attention to this matter.

Melissa Spelt

Melissa Spelt

PRESS RELEASE

Missouri Department of Education
Contact: Melissa "Missy" Spelt
November 9

For Immediate Release

Recent photo of F. Waters

WITCH HUNT BEGINS FOR FLORENCE WATERS

JEFFERSON CITY, MO—The Missouri Department of Education is seeking any information on the whereabouts of substitute teacher Florence Waters.

Officials at the Missouri Department of Education recently learned that Waters is a witch.

Attempts to reach Waters at her home in California have been unsuccessful. Anyone with information regarding her whereabouts is urged to contact the Missouri Department of Education immediately.

The Missouri Department of Education is an Equal Opportunity Employer. However, we will not tolerate witches who practice their craft during class time and/or who instruct or encourage students to cast spells and/or embalm bodies on school property.

Missouri teachers who are not practicing witches (during regular school hours) can rest assured that Ms. Waters will *not* be eligible for the HIVE Prize.

Special thanks to Mrs. Polly Nader at Springfield Middle School for alerting us to this important matter.

*　　*　　*

November 10

Florence Waters
Endangered Teacher
c/o Cave of the Spider
Valencia, Spain

Dear Florence,

Oh, man. You're not going to believe what people are saying about you.

Florence, they think you're a witch!

It's all Mrs. Nader's fault.

What makes me mad is that we wanted you to win the HIVE Prize. The winner gets $1,000,000.

But now you're not eligible because the executive director of the Missouri Department of Education says you're a witch. It's terrible when people get the wrong idea about you. I know exactly how you must feel.

Florence, they're looking everywhere for you. Please be careful!

Tad

Shelly   Lily   Paddy   Minnie O.   Gil

P.S. We've offered to teach Mr. N. sign language, but he just ignores us.

Somewhere over India

November 16

My Classy Class of Seventh Graders
Geyser Creek Middle School
Geyser Creek, Missouri USA

Dear Friends,

What terrific luck! Your letter was delivered just as I was
boarding my plane. It occurred to me that perhaps honey-
hunting strategies have changed over the last 8,000 years.

So I'm going on a contemporary honey hunt—in Malaysia!

Every November honey hunters gather in the old-growth rain
forest near Pedu Lake to search the local tualang trees for the
giant Asian honeybees (*Apis dorsata*), the world's largest and
fiercest honeybee species.

These are truly spectacular creatures, with bands of dark
orange, black, and white circling their bodies. Black fuzz
covers their heads and legs. And their black wings, when
spread, look like capes. You might think these giant bees were
mini Draculas!

Don't worry, I'll BEE careful. More from Malaysia!

Assignment enclosed. You know what to do with it.

Yours in the pursuit of honey,   *H.J. Florence*

P.S. I laughed out loud when I read that people were calling me a witch. Did you know that's *exactly* what Europeans said of the Mayan honey hunters? Mexican natives developed such a close and caring relationship with the native stingless bees in the Yucatán that Spanish colonists thought the Mayans must be *witches*.

P.P.S. I'm enclosing a BEE suit for Sam. I know he's been acting odd, but I'd still feel better if he had some protection when the BEEs arrive.

If you or he want to write to me in Malaysia, use this address:

> Florence Waters
> c/o The Tallest Tualang Tree
> Pedu Lake, Malaysia

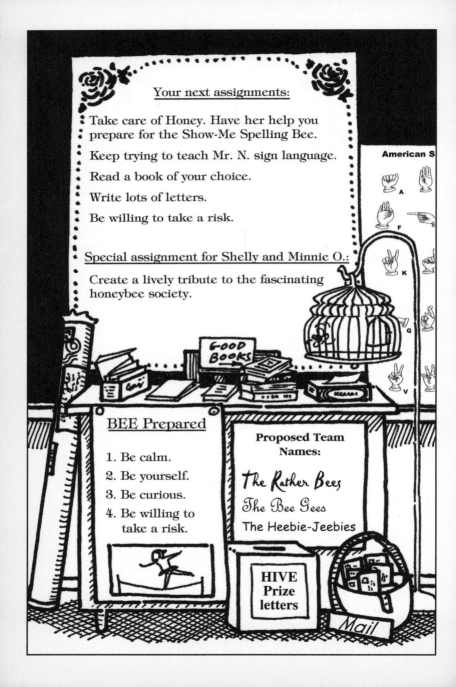

Your next assignments:

Take care of Honey. Have her help you prepare for the Show-Me Spelling Bee.

Keep trying to teach Mr. N. sign language.

Read a book of your choice.

Write lots of letters.

Be willing to take a risk.

Special assignment for Shelly and Minnie O.:

Create a lively tribute to the fascinating honeybee society.

American S

GOOD BOOKS →

BEE Prepared

1. Be calm.
2. Be yourself.
3. Be curious.
4. Be willing to take a risk.

Proposed Team Names:

The Rather Bees

The Bee Gees

The Heebie-Jeebies

HIVE Prize letters

Mail

If you could BE a BEE, what kind of BEE would you BE?

The queen

A worker bee

A drone

A honeybee colony consists of one queen, thousands of workers, and several hundred drones. Each bee has his or her clearly defined duties.

The queen begins life as an ordinary female worker larva. By feeding on royal jelly, she becomes queen. Her role is to lay eggs.

The worker bees are female honeybees. They gather pollen and nectar; feed young larvae and drones; build honeycomb; secrete beeswax—and perform many other tasks. Worker bees are the true laborers of the colony.

Drones are male honeybees. They neither collect pollen nor make beeswax. Except for mating, they are expendable members of the bee colony. Most drones are driven from the colony in late summer having done no work at all—other than mating with the queen. Drones usually die from starvation because they never learn to feed themselves.

What's the buzz on beestings?

A drone cannot sting, and the queen bee rarely stings. But the worker honeybee will sting if she feels threatened.

When a worker bee stings, her stinger is pulled from her body and she dies.

For most people, a beesting can be mildly painful but otherwise is medically insignificant. For others, a sting can produce a sudden and severe allergic reaction known as anaphylactic shock.

Sam N.
Acting Principal
Geyser Creek Middle School
Geyser Creek, Missouri

November 22

Florence Waters
c/o The Tallest Tualang Tree
Pedu Lake, Malaysia

Dear Florence,

The seventh graders passed along your current address—as well as the bee suit. Thank you.

Speaking of bees, it seems that every day there's a notice in the paper about how this year's BEEs are going to be unusually nasty. They're throwing a new species at us this time.

Anyway, just thought you should know. I'm sure you have more important things to worry about. I know I do. I'm now almost completely deaf in both ears, and Goldie is almost completely finished with me.

Sam N.

Sam N.
Acting ODD Principal
Geyser Creek Middle School
Geyser Creek, Missouri USA

November 25

Pedu Lake, Malaysia

Sam,

Exactly what kind of species
of BEEs do you expect?

Would love to chat more, but
I'm in the middle of a honey
hunt.

Florence

P.S. What do you mean
Goldie's "almost completely
finished" with you?

November 30

Florence Waters
c/o The Tallest Tualang Tree
Pedu Lake, Malaysia

Florence,

What I mean is, my relationship with Goldie is in dire condition. We're still together—for now. But I know she's looking for a new job and a new house.

It's all my fault. I haven't told her about my hearing loss. I know I should, but I just can't get up the nerve. If she knew, she'd leave me for sure.

I want to be a good husband and a good father. But how can I be if I can't hear?

Sam N.

P.S. I'm not sure what kind of BEEs we're getting. I just know they're going to be real killers this year.

Pedu Lake, Malaysia

December 3

Sam N.
Acting Principal Who, In My Humble Opinion,
    Is Acting Unbelievably Cowardly
Geyser Creek Middle School
Geyser Creek, Missouri USA

Sam,

The BEEs are killers? For heaven's sake, Sam. This changes everything!!!

If you're not going to help the students in their hour of need, will you kindly be like a bee and BUZZ off?

I have made arrangements to be in Geyser Creek the morning the BEEs arrive. The seventh graders and I will battle the BEEs without your help.

Florence

P.S. For your information, you do not need *ears* to hear. You can "listen" with your eyes, your brain, or your heart. Now stop being a coward and tell Goldie about your hearing loss.

Sam N.
Acting Principal
Geyser Creek Middle School
Geyser Creek, Missouri

December 5

Goldie Fisch-N.
Across the Office from Me
Geyser Creek Middle School
Geyser Creek, Missouri

Dear Goldie,

I can't bear to be in the same office with you when you won't talk to me or even look at me.

Goldie, can we please talk?

Sam

GEYSER CREEK MIDDLE SCHOOL
Geyser Creek, Missouri

Goldie Fisch-N.
School Secretary

December 5

Sam N.
Acting Principal
  Who Can Take His Act on the Road for All I Care
Geyser Creek Middle School
Geyser Creek, Missouri

Sam,

I'm done talking to you. I cannot work or live with someone who treats me like his stupid worker bee and refuses to listen to me.

Goldie

P.S. If you're not going to discipline the seventh graders, I am. Their classroom sounds like a zoo.

Sam N.
Acting Principal
Geyser Creek Middle School
Geyser Creek, Missouri

December 5

Goldie Fisch-N.
Across the Office from Me
Geyser Creek Middle School
Geyser Creek, Missouri

Goldie,

I'm sorry about the seventh graders. I thought everything was under control in there.

Can we please talk tonight after I get back from the Show-Me Spelling Bee?

There's something I need to tell you. It will explain why I've been such a bad listener lately.

Sam

GEYSER CREEK MIDDLE SCHOOL
Geyser Creek, Missouri

Goldie Fisch-N.
School Secretary

December 5

Sam,

You won't even listen to me when I *write* to you.

Our marriage is over. Please don't come home tonight after the Show-Me Spelling Bee.

Goldie

P. S. Sam, I'm sorry if
this is painful for you.
If you only knew how
much it hurts

GEYSER CREEK
AMBULANCE SERVICE DISPATCH

1:25 P.M.

December 5

EMERGENCY MEDICAL TEAM NEEDED IMMEDIATELY AT GEYSER CREEK MIDDLE SCHOOL.

SCHOOL SECRETARY COLLAPSED IN OFFICE. SEVEN MONTHS PREGNANT. DOESN'T SOUND GOOD.

✶THE GEYSER CREEK GAZETTE✶

Our motto: "We have a nose for news!"

Monday, December 5   **Late Edition**   50 cents

Goldie Fisch-N. Rushed to Hospital

By Tad Poll, Special Correspondent

Geyser Creek Middle School secretary Goldie Fisch-N. was rushed to the intensive care unit (ICU) at Geyser Creek Memorial Hospital at approximately 1:30 p.m. today after she collapsed at her desk while writing a stinging note to her husband.

"Goldie's condition is critical," said Sandy Beech, MD.

Fisch-N. is seven months pregnant. Her husband, Acting Principal Sam N., accompanied his wife to the hospital in the ambulance.

"We warned Sam that the sirens were loud, but he said he didn't care," said Geyser Creek Emergency Director Justin Case.

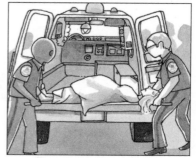

**Emergency workers transport
Goldie Fisch-N. from school.**

Witch Hunt Continues for Substitute Teacher

**Melissa Spelt plans to fire Waters when
the famous designer arrives for the BEEs.**

The top official with the Missouri Department of Education continued her search for Geyser Creek Middle School substitute teacher Florence Waters, an alleged witch.

"We are reviewing her recent correspondence and planning a sting operation," said Melissa "Missy" Spelt, who arrived yesterday in Geyser Creek. "It appears Waters will be in Geyser Creek tomorrow for the Basic Education Evaluation. We will present her with termination papers, and then kindly request that

she return to California and have no further contact with the children of Missouri."

In other news, Spelt said that the winner of the Highly Innovative and Victorious Educator (HIVE) Prize will be announced on January 1. Although Spelt refused to give any clues about the identity of the winner, she did say: "I'll tell you who it *won't* be: Florence Waters."

Important Notice

The Basic Education Evaluation (BEE) is tomorrow.

ALL Missouri middle school students are required to take the BEE.

Remember: During the BEEs, teachers may NOT assist students in any way, shape or form.

The Show-Me Spelling Bee Must Go On

Their principal is out of town.

Their regular teacher, who's serving as acting principal, is in the hospital with his critically ill wife.

Their substitute teacher is on the lam.

And Honey, their real-live spelling bee, has been disqualified.

But the seventh-grade students at Geyser Creek Middle School say they have no plans to pull out of tonight's Show-Me Spelling Bee in Springfield.

"We might not win," said Shelly, "but we'll never know if we don't try. Sometimes you just have to take a risk. That's what Florence told us."

The students received a letter earlier today from substitute teacher Florence Waters, who wished them luck in the Show-Me Spelling Bee. In the letter, postmarked from Pedu Lake, Malaysia, Waters wrote: "Do your best and don't be afraid to fail. Remember, you always lose if you never try. Just wing it, dears! And don't forget to take Honey for good luck."

The Geyser Creek seventh graders completed an earlier assignment from Waters by deciding on a team name.

"We're calling ourselves the Let It Bees," said Gil. "The name reflects our philosophy."

Geyser Creek seventh graders will attend spelling bee tonight.

GEYSER CREEK MEMORIAL HOSPITAL

December 5
9:15 P.M.

Dear Goldie,

I'm writing this to you from the crowded waiting room of the ICU, where, ironically, I'm not allowed to C U at all.

All I can do is sit here with a heart as heavy as an anchor while I wait for news from the doctors about you and our baby.

Goldie, there's something I've wanted to tell you for months. It's the reason why I've seemed so distant lately. You thought that I was ignoring you, but the truth is—

Ugh. Someone just turned on the TV.

People are gathering around to watch something. Oh, I see. The Show-Me Spelling Bee is on. Hey, there's Tad! He's . . . never mind. He was just eliminated on the word *penultimate*. Now a Springfield Middle School student is up. He just spelled *onomatopoeia* correctly. Now he's giving Polly Nader a big smile. Looks like the Yellow Jackets have this thing wrapped up. Wait. Shelly's still in. Good for her! Go, Shelly!!!

Why am I watching closed-captioned TV when I should be writing to the woman I love?

Goldie, I don't care about spelling bees. I don't care about bees that can spell. The only things I care about are you, our relationship, and our baby. That's why I've been so afraid to tell you something. I think it might change the way you feel about me. I don't know what I'd do if I ever lost you, Goldie. But I have to be honest and tell you that I . . .

What the *heck*? Everyone in the waiting room is jumping up and down. Something's happened at the Show-Me Spelling Bee. *Huh?* What?!! Goldie, you're not going to believe this!!

EXCERPT FROM TV TRANSCRIPT

JUDGE: As we enter the 56th round of the Show-Me Spelling Bee, only two students remain: Horace Fly, representing the Yellow Jackets from Springfield Middle School, and Shelly from the Let It Bees at Geyser Creek Middle School. Shelly, are you ready?

SHELLY: I am, sir.

JUDGE: Your word is *drone*.

SHELLY: May I have a definition, please?

JUDGE: A drone is a male bee that does no work, produces no honey, and is incapable of stinging. *Drone* can also mean a loafer or sluggard. Used as a verb, *drone* means to make a low, dull humming sound.

SHELLY: Drone. D-R-O-N-E.

JUDGE: That is correct.

[SOUND OF APPLAUSE]

JUDGE: Horace, your turn. Are you ready?

HORACE FLY: Yeah, whatever.

JUDGE: Your word is *anaphylactic*.

HORACE FLY: Oh, gimme a big fat break! Geyser Creek gets *drone* and I get this?

JUDGE: Your attitude could get you eliminated from the competition, young man.

POLLY NADER: Oh, Judge, Horace doesn't mean it. He's just so excited by the—*ahem*—task at hand.

JUDGE: No comments from the audience. Sit down, Mrs. Nader, or I'll disqualify your student. The word is *anaphylactic*.

HORACE FLY: A-N-A—

[SOUND OF SCREAM]

JUDGE: What is it now?

POLLY NADER: There's a bee in here!

MINNIE O.: Sorry! Honey got out of her cage. Don't worry. She won't hurt you unless she feels—

JUDGE: Quiet in the audience! We're in the middle of a word. Please continue.

HORACE FLY: P-Z-X-L-Y-B. Mrs. Nader, I can't tell what you're doing!

POLLY NADER: I'm trying to get this bee away from me!

HORACE FLY: R-M-L-C-T-W-D-F-Q-O-U.

POLLY NADER: Shut up, you idiot!

HORACE FLY: But that's what you just spelled.

POLLY NADER: I'm not spelling! I'm trying to protect myself from—*yeowch!*

HORACE FLY: R-S-B-N-M-A-Q-Q-L-M-Z-B.

JUDGE: Are you quite finished, young man?

HORACE FLY: Are we finished, Mrs. Nader? Mrs. Nader?

POLLY NADER: [SOUND OF FAINT WHIMPERING]

JUDGE: It appears your teacher is in anaphylactic shock, young man. Shelly, can you spell *anaphylactic*?

SHELLY: A-N-A-P-H-Y-L-A-C-T-I-C.

JUDGE: Correct. If you can spell the next word correctly, the Let It Bees will be the winners.

SHELLY (breathlessly): T-H-E N-E-X-T W-O-R-D C-O-R-R-E-C-T-L-Y.

JUDGE: We have a winner! Now somebody call an ambulance for Mrs. Nader.

HORACE FLY: But that's not fair! Mrs. Nader was doing all kind of weird things, and I couldn't tell—

JUDGE: Couldn't tell what?

HORACE FLY: Um . . . Er . . . I can't tell.

LILY: Well, I can.

PADDY: I can, too.

MINNIE O.: And so can I.

TAD POLL: Me, too.

SHELLY: I say we call a press conference.

GIL: And tell the whole world that the Yellow Jackets are a bunch of—

LET IT BEES: D-I-R-T-Y R-O-T-T-E-N C-H-E-A-T-E-R-S!

✶ THE GEYSER CREEK GAZETTE ✶

Our motto: "We have a nose for news!"

Tuesday, December 6   **Early Edition**   **50 cents**

Very IntereSTING!
Polly Nader Nabbed in Cheating Scandal

By Tad Poll, Special Correspondent

A spellbinding turn of events has left Springfield Middle School teacher Polly Nader fired, hospitalized and disqualified from the HIVE Prize competition.

The drama began at last night's Show-Me Spelling Bee when a honeybee escaped from its cage and made an honest-to-goodness beeline for Nader, who waved her arms frantically in an attempt to shoo the bee away.

Unfortunately for Nader, her wild hand gestures were misinterpreted by her student Horace Fly, who thought Nader was telling him in sign language how to spell the word *anaphylactic*.

Anaphylactic was the penultimate spelling word in last night's competition. *Anaphylactic* also describes the severe allergic reaction suffered by Nader when she was stung by Honey, the spelling bee.

Nader was rushed to Springfield Hospital, where she was met by Melissa Spelt, executive director of the Missouri Department of

Springfield teacher caught in hive of controversy.

Education. After Geyser Creek Middle School custodian Sugar Kube confirmed that Nader was using American Sign Language, Spelt fired Nader on the spot for helping her students cheat in the Show-Me Spelling Bee and on the Basic Education Evaluation. (See related story, below.)

Spelt also officially called off the witch hunt for substitute teacher Florence Waters.

Teacher's Pest Tells All

By Tad Poll, Special Correspondent

While reporters swarmed around him, Horace Fly explained how his teacher, Polly Nader, used American Sign Language to help him and his classmates win last year's Show-Me Spelling Bee and ace the Basic Education Evaluation (BEE).

"Mrs. Nader sat in the audience and spelled the words for us with her hands," said Fly. "It was pretty much the same thing with the BEEs. She'd stand in the front of the classroom and tell us the answers in sign language."

Fly said Nader also wrote letters of recommendation, nominating herself for the Highly Innovative and Victorious Educator (HIVE) Prize. She forced her students to copy the letters in their own handwriting and send them

Horace Fly reveals Yellow Jackets' secret to success.

to HIVE Prize judge Melissa Spelt.

"Mrs. Nader promised us if she won, we'd get 10 percent of the HIVE Prize money," said Fly.

According to Fly, Nader also told her students she had to win the HIVE Prize so she could retire early.

"She really hated teaching," said Fly. "Or maybe she just hated kids. She was a real witch."

BEE Czar Predicts Bad BEE Scores

By Tad Poll, Special Correspondent

The thrill of last night's victory at the Show-Me Spelling Bee by the Let It Bees at Geyser Creek Middle School was tempered by the agony of their expected defeat today by the Basic Education Evaluation (BEE).

"With all the running around these students have been doing, I predict record-low test scores for the seventh-grade students at Geyser Creek Middle School," said BEE director Benny Bob "B. B." King.

King said he predicted BEE scores from Mrs. Polly Nader's seventh-grade class at Springfield Middle School will be dismal, too.

"With Polly Nader in the hospital, it will be interesting to see how her students do on the BEEs," King said.

For several months King has been warning that this year's BEE will be the most challenging test in years.

The victorious Let It Bees return home after winning the Show-Me Spelling Bee.

Bee Sweet!

Goldie wanted me to thank everyone who sent flowers and good wishes to her in the hospital. She's feeling okay, but the doctors say her condition is still critical. And Sam, if you're reading this, Goldie still wants you to move out.
—Angel Fisch

P.S. to Sam: I forget to tell you something, my friend. You cannot watch the TV when your wife, she is sick as the dogs.
—Chef Angelo

Have you experienced an unusual act of sweetness?
If so, we want to know about it.
Send your Bee Sweet stories to:
The *Gazette*, Geyser Creek, Mo.

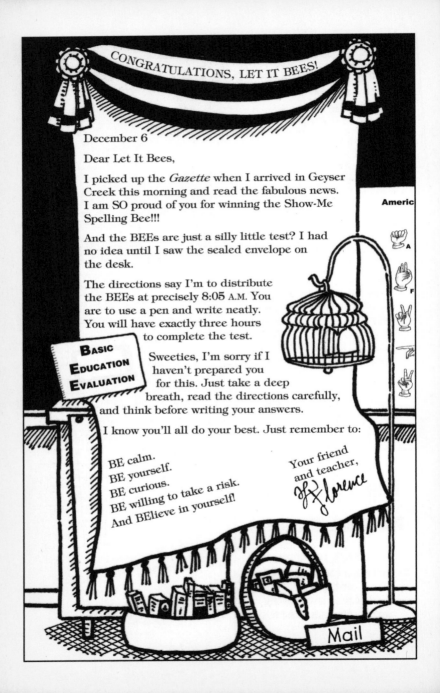

CONGRATULATIONS, LET IT BEES!

December 6

Dear Let It Bees,

I picked up the *Gazette* when I arrived in Geyser Creek this morning and read the fabulous news. I am SO proud of you for winning the Show-Me Spelling Bee!!!

And the BEEs are just a silly little test? I had no idea until I saw the sealed envelope on the desk.

The directions say I'm to distribute the BEEs at precisely 8:05 A.M. You are to use a pen and write neatly. You will have exactly three hours to complete the test.

Sweeties, I'm sorry if I haven't prepared you for this. Just take a deep breath, read the directions carefully, and think before writing your answers.

I know you'll all do your best. Just remember to:

BE calm.
BE yourself.
BE curious.
BE willing to take a risk.
And BElieve in yourself!

Your friend and teacher,

Florence

BASIC
EDUCATION
EVALUATION

Americ

Mail

BASIC EDUCATION EVALUATION
(BEE)

This year's BEE consists of just one question.

In the space provided, discuss your personal interpretation of the famous line from William Shakespeare's play *Hamlet:* "To be, or not to be: that is the question."

_____
_____
_____
_____
_____
_____
_____
_____
_____
_____
_____
_____
_____
_____
_____
_____
_____
_____
_____
_____
_____
_____
_____
_____
_____
_____
_____
_____

December 12

Mr. Sam N.
Acting Principal
Geyser Creek Middle School
Geyser Creek, Missouri

<u>Regarding the BEEs</u>

Dear Mr. N.,

I have just received the results for this year's BEEs. Congratulations. All the students in the seventh-grade class at Geyser Creek Middle School received perfect scores.

As you may have heard, this year's BEE was an essay test. It was designed to frustrate those who teach to the test—and others, like Mrs. Polly Nader, who simply cheat.

Although many students across the state found the essay format difficult, your students rose to the occasion. One of your seventh graders interpreted Shakespeare's words *"To be, or not to be"* as the challenge of self-definition. Other students wrote their essays about beekeeping, pointing out the cooperative nature of the hive. Another Geyser Creek seventh grader waxed poetic about how studying the dance of honeybees taught him how "to bee" a better dancer. Yet another student wrote a compelling narrative about the anxiety of being misunderstood. She used the example of prehistoric honey hunters and compared them to contemporary young people in pursuit of romance.

Perhaps the most surprising essay of all came from a student named Gil, who correctly placed the quote within the context of *Hamlet* and eloquently discussed the character's anguished state in act 3, scene 1 of the play. This essay could be published.

Whatever you and your staff did to prepare the students for the BEE is to be applauded.

Sincerely,

B. B. King
BEE Czar

GEYSER CREEK MEMORIAL HOSPITAL

December 13

Florence Waters
Geyser Creek B & B
43 Honeysuckle Lane
Geyser Creek, Missouri

Dear Florence,

I am enclosing a copy of a letter I just received from the director of the Basic Education Evaluation.

As far as I know, the seventh graders have never studied "self-definition" or Shakespeare—and surely not prehistoric honey hunters. I don't think they prepared at all for the BEEs.

It's a mystery to me how they could've scored so high on the BEEs—unless you saw the test before you arrived in Geyser Creek and tipped them off. Or maybe you helped the students write their essays.

Florence, this is unbearably awkward to ask, but I have to know: Did you help the students on the BEEs?

Please respond by letter as I am now completely deaf in both ears. I am also camping in the ICU waiting room, hoping Goldie will change her mind about seeing me.

Sincerely,

Sam N.

December 14

Sam N.
Acting Principal Who's Now Just Acting Silly
c/o Geyser Creek Memorial Hospital
Geyser Creek, Missouri

Oh, Sam.

Now you're really starting to sound like an administrative
drone.

Of course I didn't help the seventh graders cheat. Not my
style. Did it ever occur to you that perhaps *you* prepared the
students for the BEEs—simply by providing them with a safe
place to study and play, and then letting them *be*? You saw
the students as neither pests nor threats. Instead, you wisely
admired them for their natural industry. In short, you treated
them just like bees!

As with teaching, few people go into beekeeping for the
money. For most of us, it's the love of these small creatures,
though they can be difficult and—yes, at times—even a tiny
bit painful. But golly, they're fun to watch. And the fruit of
their labor is sweet indeed!

Sam, I've been wondering: Like a good beekeeper, in addition
to producing some fine honeys, have you also collected a lot
of wax . . . in your ears? Could *that* be the source of your
hearing loss?

Or should I mind my own beeswax?   *Florence*

GEYSER CREEK MEMORIAL HOSPITAL

HAND DELIVERED

December 15

Florence Waters
Geyser Creek B & B
43 Honeysuckle Lane
Geyser Creek, Missouri

Florence!

How in the world did you know?! Never mind.

You're a lifesaver. And a marriage saver, too.

Thank you!

Sam N.

December 16

Florence Waters
A Real Honey of a Substitute Teacher
Flowing Waters Fountains, Etc.
Watertown, California

Dear Florence,

You left town before we got a chance to tell you the good news about the BEEs. Would you believe we all got perfect scores? We owe it to you. Thanks for encouraging us to believe in ourselves and take risks. I took a risk and told everybody I wanted to have a class dance on New Year's Eve. I even offered to teach everyone how to dance like a bee.

Then I took a risk and told Tad I thought it was a great idea. I also said I'd like to go to the dance with him, if Gil didn't mind.

I said sure. Then I took a risk and told everybody that I don't want to start dating yet.

So then I took a risk and told Gil that we didn't have to be boyfriend and girlfriend. But I'd sure like to be friends with him, if Shelly didn't mind.

It's fine with me!

I guess being friends would be okay.

That leaves only Paddy and me. We still don't have

boyfriends. And worse than that, we feel too guilty to go to a dance. Florence, we took a risk and planned that sting operation at the Show-Me Spelling Bee. But we forgot one thing: After Honey stung Mrs. Nader, our little spelling bee died. Talk about a buzz kill.

Honey was such a sweet bee. She actually winked at us and spelled <u>Good-bye</u> right before she stung Mrs. Nader and died. Oh, Florence. We're so sorry. Will you ever forgive us?

Sincerely,

Tad

Shelly

Gil

Minnie O.

Lily

Paddy

Watertown, California

December 17

Seventh-Grade Correspondence Class
Geyser Creek Middle School
Geyser Creek, Missouri

Dear Sweeties,

Of course I can believe you all got As on the BEEs! And to think I thought they were killer bees!

Well, I can think of $329\frac{1}{2}$ things that are more fun to do than taking tests. But there's nothing better than a test of any kind to show what kind of person you are. Are you honest, or are you someone who cheats? Are you willing to try your best in any situation, even if it means you might not win? Or do you quit at the first sign of trouble?

The exciting thing is that *you* get to decide what kind of person you're going to be. To be or not to be: That is the FUN question! (And do you want to know a secret? I don't care what scores you get on tests as long as you meet every challenge with honor.)

I've enclosed your final assignments for the semester.

Un*BEE*lievably proud
           to BE
               your friend,

H. Florence

P.S. to Lily and Paddy: I know you're sorry about Honey. I am, too. But I also know that bees are by nature one of the most self-sacrificing creatures on Earth. Like you, they attack only when attacked, and only to defend themselves and their close-knit community. I'm confident that Honey was proud to sacrifice her life for your honor. Maybe you'd feel better if you could find a way to honor Honey in return.

P.P.S. And for goodness' sake, girls, you don't need boyfriends to go to a dance. Life is not about who you're with but who you *are*.

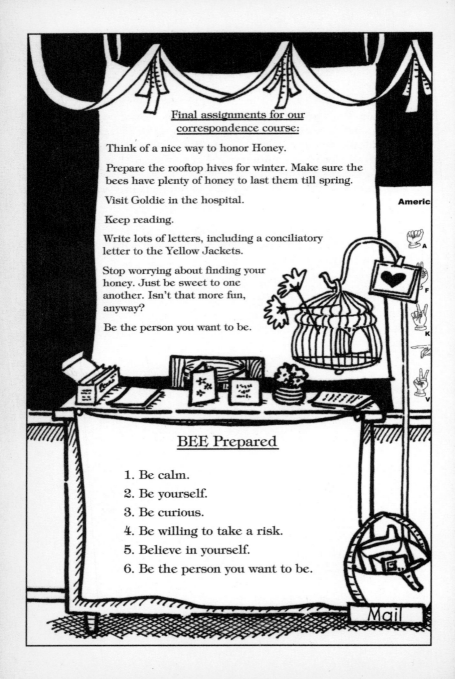

<u>Final assignments for our</u>
<u>correspondence course:</u>

Think of a nice way to honor Honey.

Prepare the rooftop hives for winter. Make sure the bees have plenty of honey to last them till spring.

Visit Goldie in the hospital.

Keep reading.

Write lots of letters, including a conciliatory letter to the Yellow Jackets.

Stop worrying about finding your honey. Just be sweet to one another. Isn't that more fun, anyway?

Be the person you want to be.

Americ

A

F

K

V

<u>BEE Prepared</u>

1. Be calm.
2. Be yourself.
3. Be curious.
4. Be willing to take a risk.
5. Believe in yourself.
6. Be the person you want to be.

Mail

December 19

The Yellow Jackets
Springfield Middle School
Springfield, Missouri

Dear Yellow Jackets,

We were very sorry to hear about your record-low scores on the BEEs.

And too bad your teacher got fired.

We hope you get a nice substitute teacher, like the one we had this semester.

Hey, we were wondering: Do you want to be pen pals with our class?

Writing letters is a fun way to get to know people. Plus, it might help improve your scores on next year's BEEs.

We'd also like to invite you to our school on New Year's Eve. We've enclosed an invitation.

Sincerely,

Lily

Gil

Shelly

Minnie O.

Paddy

Tad Poll

You Are Cordially Invited

To Bee or Not to Bee

That Is the Name
of the

Dance

We Are Having
on *New Year's Eve*
at Geyser Creek Middle School

to Honor
the Memory of Our Friend

HONEY,

the Spelling Bee,

Who Taught Us
So Much About
Spelling,
Dating,
Sacrifice,
Community,
as well as
the Art of the Sting!

Please come alone, with a friend, a date, or in a group.

Kindly RSVP to the
Let It Bees
Seventh-Grade Correspondence Class
Geyser Creek Middle School
Geyser Creek, Missouri

THE YELLOW JACKETS

~~Mrs. Polly Nader's Seventh Grade Class~~
Springfield Middul School
Springfield, Misery

Desemmbur 21

Let It Bees
Seventh Grade Corruspondunce Class
Geyser Creak Middul School
Geyser Creak, Misery

Deer Let It Bees,

Okay. We'll come too the dance.

But onlee if you promice not too make fun of us four being sent back two fif grade.

Sin-sara-lee,

Maureen ("Moe") Skitto

P. Daddy Longlegs   Horace Fly

P.S. Being pen pals soundz like fun. May bee you can also teech us about be keeping. And sppeling.

☆ THE GEYSER CREEK GAZETTE ☆

Our motto: "We have a nose for news!"

Sunday, January 1   **Early Edition**   **$1.00**

How Do You Spell HIVE Prize Winner?
G-E-Y-S-E-R C-R-E-E-K M-I-D-D-L-E S-C-H-O-O-L

By Tad Poll, Special Correspondent

The school will use prize money for apiary and weekly dances.

Drumroll, please!

This year's Highly Innovative and Victorious Educator (HIVE) Prize goes to . . . Geyser Creek Middle School.

"After the students in the seventh-grade class won the Show-Me Spelling Bee and scored highest on the Basic Education Evaluation, it was clear the prize should go to someone at that school," explained Melissa Spelt, executive director of the Missouri Department of Education and HIVE Prize judge. "The only question was *who*?"

Spelt said that the seventh-grade students at Geyser Creek Middle School nominated substitute teacher Florence Waters, who in turn nominated Acting Principal Sam N., saying that he was the true educator at the school.

According to Spelt, Sam N. nominated his wife, Goldie Fisch-N., saying that she had taught him about the importance of good communication in a relationship.

"The only solution was to give the HIVE Prize to the entire Geyser Creek Middle School community," said Spelt. "After all, this is a school that functions very much like a hive. The staff and students have created a community that's not only productive, collaborative and social but that also values working in harmony with one another and in sync with the rhythms of nature."

Acting Principal Sam N. said his students and staff had taken a vote and decided to spend a portion of the $1 million prize money to build a school apiary, patterned after the rooftop apiary at the Palais Garnier, an old opera house in Paris. The remaining funds will be used to host a school dance every Saturday night.

"We're going to call it the Weekly Correspond Dance," said Lily, a seventh grader. "It's inspired by our friend and teacher, Florence Waters, who encouraged our class to correspond weekly."

"She also helped me learn to dance," added this reporter.

To Bee or Not to Bee

Either Way, First Weekly Correspond Dance Was a Lot of Fun

By Tad Poll, Special Correspondent

Last night's To Bee or Not to Bee dance was the first in a series of Weekly Correspond Dances to be held at Geyser Creek Middle School.

The free social event was planned by seventh-grade students, who invited the entire town.

"We want everyone in Geyser Creek to come to our weekly dances," said Paddy.

The students served punch and cookies at the dance, which was romantically lit with beeswax candles made by the seventh graders' bees.

As a precaution Geyser Creek Fire Marshal Whitey Bass was on hand with fire hoses.

"You can never be too careful with candles—or seventh graders," said Bass, who admitted he'd received a request from some parents to be at the dance, "just in case the dancing got a little too, you know, steamy."

The seventh graders assured both Bass and their parents that they needn't worry about either scenario. After much deliberation the classmates decided to attend the dance as a group, rather than in couples.

"We thought it'd be more fun that way," said Shelly. "And it was!"

By far the most popular dance partner was

The first Weekly Correspond Dance was sweetly lit by beeswax candles.

Florence Waters does "the waggle" with seventh graders and Sugar Kube.

Florence Waters, who returned to Geyser Creek for last night's festivities.

"When it comes to fun, Geyser Creek is the place to *bee*!" said Waters.

Polly Nader Sentenced to House Arrest

Springfield Middle School teacher Polly Nader, formerly queen of the BEEs, has been fired and sentenced to house arrest.

"We don't want her to have any contact with children," said Melissa "Missy" Spelt, executive director of the Missouri Department of Education.

Nader has also been ordered to write 100 letters a day to her former students, whom she forced to write letters on her behalf as a contender for the HIVE Prize.

"If she doesn't want to be their pen pal,

we'll see that she's sent to the penitentiary," said Spelt. "She can see how she likes that *pen*."

To prevent Nader from leaving her home, education officials have surrounded the former teacher's house with thousands of bees.

Nader is highly allergic to bees. One sting left untreated could kill her. Just the sight of the swarming bees is proving problematic for Nader. The teacher who was expected to receive the HIVE Prize now has a terrible case of hives.

Pearl Wins Do Bee with Beehive Hairdo

Geyser Creek hairstylist Pearl O. Ster won last night's National Do Bee in New York City by creating a contemporary beehive hairdo.

Ster says she got the idea to create the hairdo while watching the Show-Me Spelling Bee on TV.

"When I saw Honey go after Polly Nader, I just had this creative burst of inspiration," said Ster. "Then when I heard about all of Nader's shenanigans, I thought, *Oh honey, have I got a do for you.*"

Ster received special permission to use Polly Nader as a hair model.

Geyser Creek's First Baby of the New Year: May Bea Fisch-N.

Goldie Fisch-N. and Sam N. welcomed their first child to the world this morning at one minute after midnight.

Born six weeks prematurely, the baby girl weighed 5 pounds, 10 ounces.

"We named her May Beatrice Fisch-N.," said Goldie Fisch-N. "But we plan to call her May Bea. It was my adorable husband's idea."

After a rocky semester, Goldie Fisch-N. finally reconciled with Sam N., who suffered a temporary hearing loss in recent months due to wax buildup in his ears.

An emergency ear irrigation procedure solved the problem for Sam N., who was at his wife's bedside for the 32 hours she was in labor.

The couple admired their new baby in the glow of beeswax candles provided by the seventh-grade class.

"It was the best date of my life," said Goldie Fisch-N.

Mother, father and baby enjoy a candlelit date in the hospital.

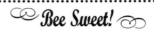

GEYSER CREEK MIDDLE SCHOOL

Geyser Creek, Missouri

Sam N.
Seventh-Grade Teacher

January 9

Mr. Walter Russ
Principal
Geyser Creek Middle School
Geyser Creek, Missouri

Welcome back, Mr. Russ.

After serving as principal for the fall semester, I have
greater respect for you and your job—though I must
disagree with you on one point: Silence *isn't* golden. To
my ears, there's nothing more beautiful than the sound
of children's voices.

Speaking of which, I hope you don't mind that I've added
a nursery next to your office. Goldie and I want to bring
our baby to school with us. Angel and Angelo do, too.
Their baby is due a month from today.

I hope this is okay with you, sir. There's a lot of work to
do with a baby. I want to make sure I'm pulling my
weight—and not being a worthless drone.

Sam N.

Sam N.

P.S. That noise you hear is the seventh graders. They're
working in the new apiary—on the school roof.

GEYSER CREEK MIDDLE SCHOOL
Geyser Creek, Missouri

Mr. Walter Russ
Principal

January 10

Mr. Sam N.
Seventh-Grade Teacher
Geyser Creek Middle School
Geyser Creek, Missouri

Mr. N.,

An apiary on the roof? A *nursery*—next to my office?

Well, I suppose we can try it.

One question: There's a large box on my desk from Florence Waters. It's emitting a low humming noise. Do you have any idea what it might . . .

Oh. Never mind. I think I know.

I'll carry it up to the roof myself.

Walter Russ

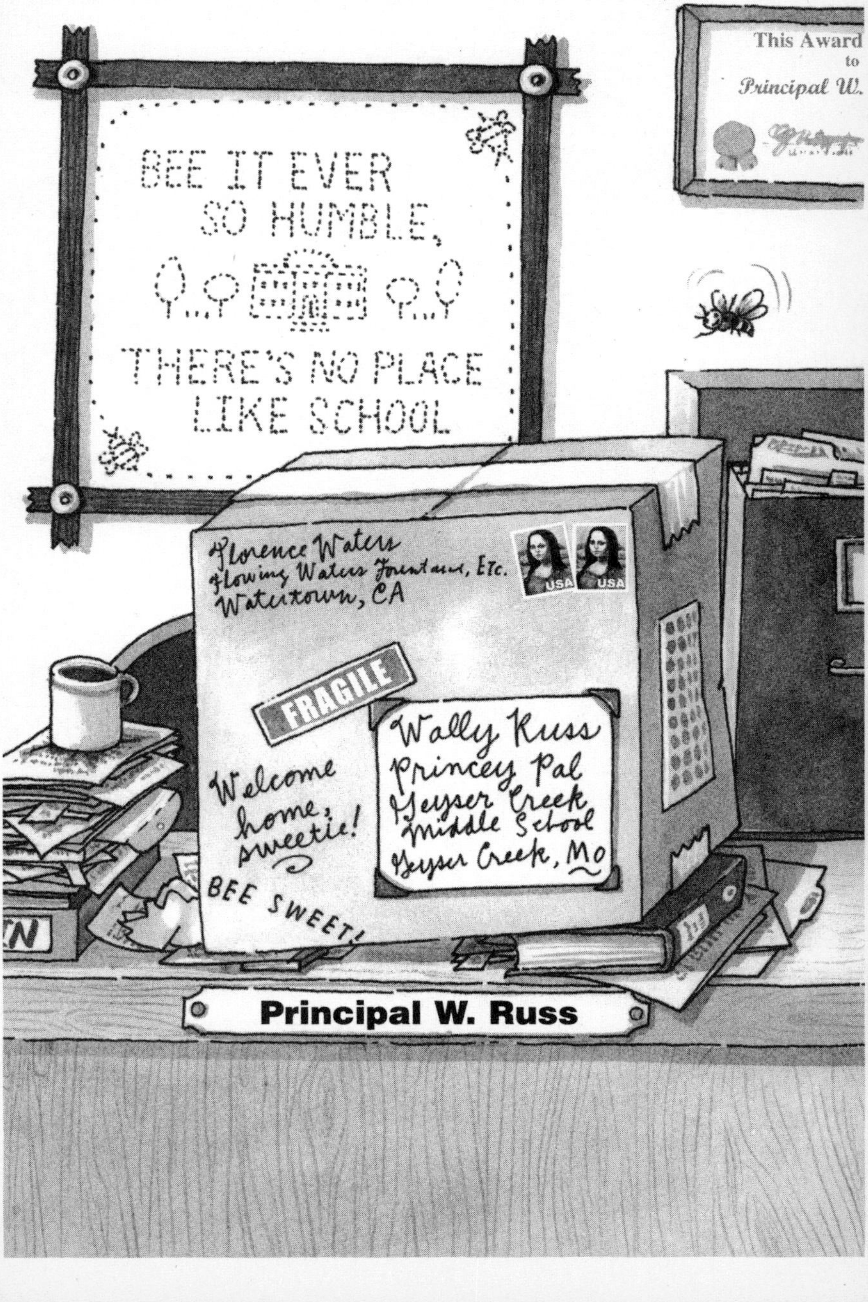
BEE IT EVER SO HUMBLE, THERE'S NO PLACE LIKE SCHOOL
This Award
to
Principal W.
Florence Waters
Flowing Waters Fountains, Etc.
Watertown, CA
USA
USA
FRAGILE
Wally Russ
Princey Pal
Geyser Creek
Middle School
Geyser Creek, Mo
Welcome home, sweetie!
BEE SWEET!
Principal W. Russ

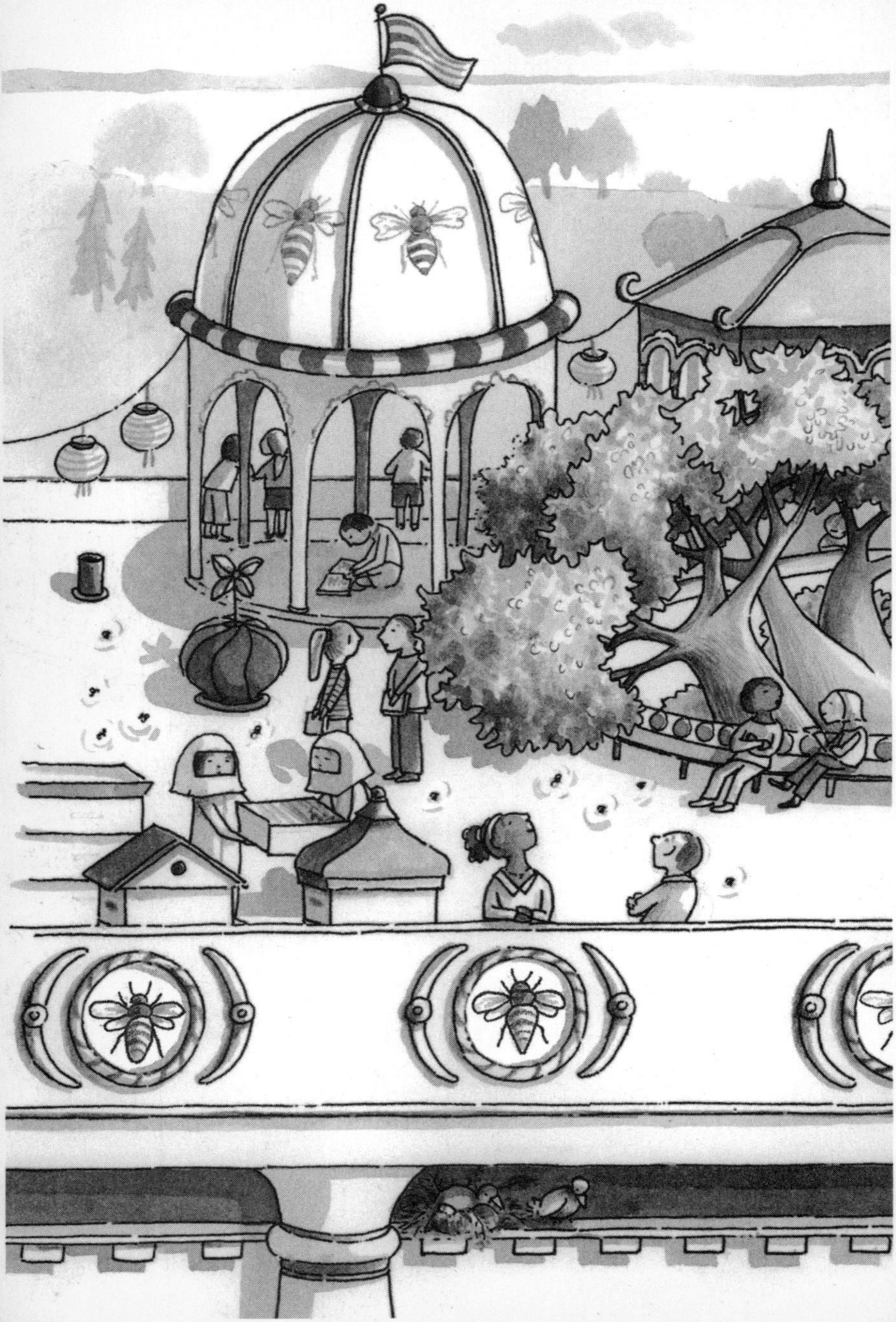

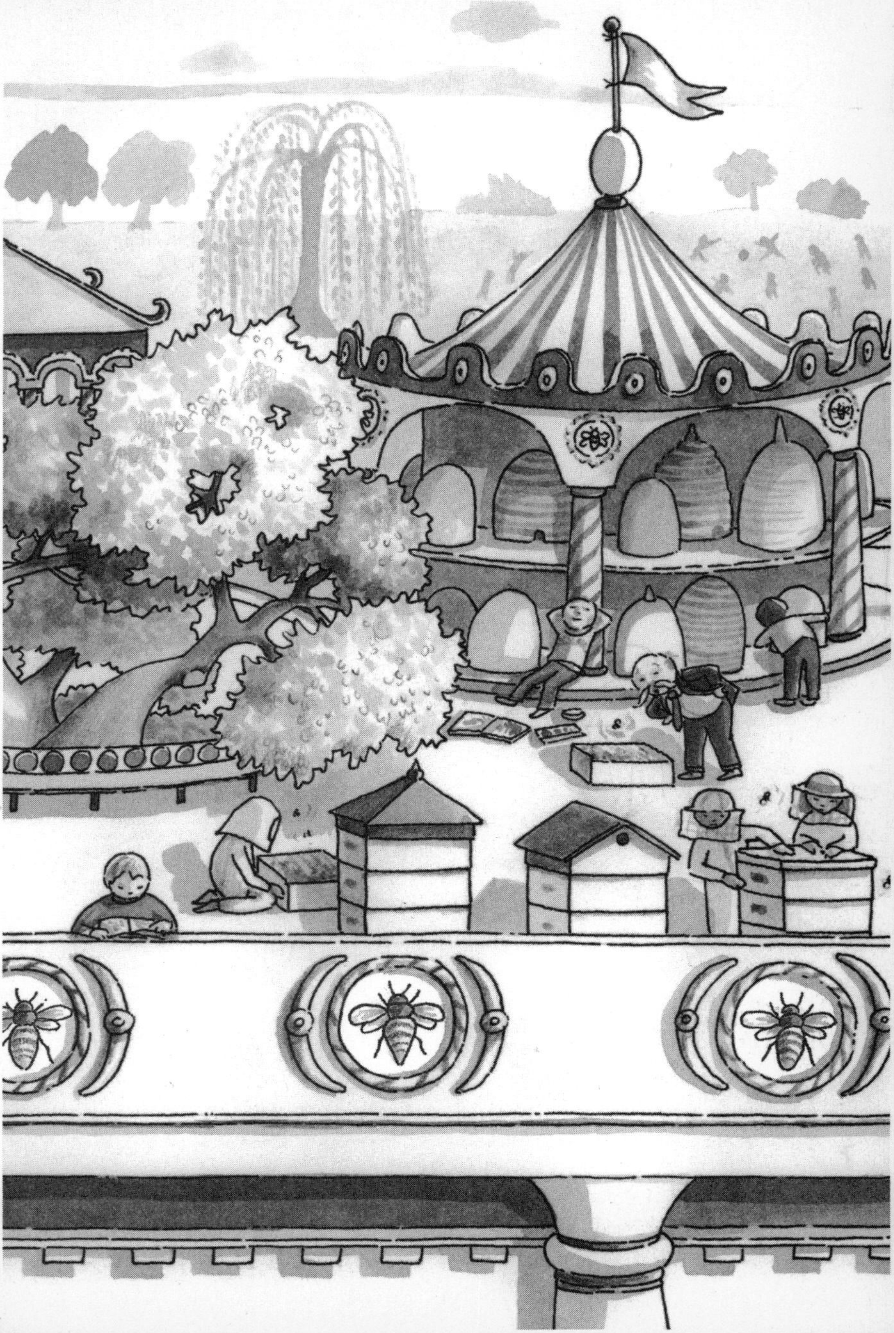

DON'T MISS THE OTHER BOOKS
IN THE REGARDING THE...SERIES!

REGARDING THE FOUNTAIN

REGARDING THE SINK

REGARDING THE TREES

REGARDING THE BATHROOMS

REGARDING THE BEES

Author **Kate Klise** (left) lives, writes, and keeps several hives of bees (yes, really!) in a little valley near Norwood, Missouri. Illustrator **M. Sarah Klise** lives, draws, and gets her honey from a store in Berkeley, California. The Klise sisters' previous collaborations include four other books in the Regarding the ... series, as well as the graphic novels *Letters from Camp* and *Trial by Journal* and the picture books *Shall I Knit You a Hat?*, *Why Do You Cry?*, and *Imagine Harry*.

To learn more about these admittedly *beezarre* sisters, make a *bee*line to their website, **www.kateandsarahklise.com**.

ACTIVITIES FOR
REGARDING THE BEES

LANGUAGE

Homophones are words that are spelled differently and have different definitions but are pronounced the same, for example, *their, they're,* and *there; bee* and *be;* and *to, too,* and *two.* Have each student make a list of homophones that appear in the book. Then have each student use the homophones correctly in a sentence. How are homophones different from homonyms?

From your school library, check out some books about American Sign Language. As a class, or in small groups, have students attempt to learn the ASL alphabet and other basic words such as *hello, thank you,* and *please.*

Organize a spelling bee with another class. Have each class select a team name.

SOCIAL STUDIES

There is a real movement throughout the United States and elsewhere called Random Acts of Kindness (www.actsofkindness.org). As a class, list random acts of kindness that will affect another class, cafeteria workers, the principal, or a school bus driver.

Throughout the book, Florence keeps adding ideas to the BEE

Prepared list. Do the students think her advice is good? Would the class add or delete any idea?

GEOGRAPHY

On a world map, pinpoint the location of Malaysia. Ask the students what is unique about the geography and shape of this country.

Give each student a political map of the world. Instruct the students to use the map to label and draw Florence Water's trip, which begins and ends in Missouri.

SCIENCE

Polly Nader is stung by a bee and has an anaphylactic reaction to the sting (pp. 100–102). Instruct the class to research anaphylactic shock. What other substances besides bee venom can cause this reaction? How is anaphylactic shock treated? Do any students have bee allergies or other allergies?

Define the word *apiary* for the class. Have the students research bees and their hives. How do bees communicate? How do they find flowers? How do bees collect pollen? How is pollen turned into honey? What are the roles of the queen and drone bees? If there is an apiary in your community, plan a class trip to see the bees and bee farmer in action.

WRITING

Mr. N's students decide to use their HIVE prize money to build an apiary and to have school dances (p. 18). For a